Here's the thing, though: if you asked me, I might have said, even then, that I know deep down that it just wasn't going to be that easy to get out. There's this old trilogy of movies called *The Godfather*. They are some of my favorite movies because they kind of remind me of Vince and me. In fact, the first time I saw them, I had to double-check what year they had come out because I could have sworn the guys who wrote that movie had stolen some of my business tricks. Anyways, in the third movie, the main character says, "Just when I thought I was out, they pull me back in."

I just hoped it wasn't the same deal for me. Where the only way out was either in handcuffs or a body bag.

**BOOKS BY**

Chris Rylander

THE FOURTH STALL SAGA
The Fourth Stall
The Fourth Stall Part II
The Fourth Stall Part III

THE CODENAME CONSPIRACY
Book 1: Codename Zero

Chris Rylander

# The Fourth Stall

## PART III

WALDEN POND PRESS

*An Imprint of HarperCollinsPublishers*

Walden Pond Press is an imprint of HarperCollins Publishers.
Walden Pond Press and the skipping stone logo are trademarks and
registered trademarks of Walden Media, LLC.

The Fourth Stall Part III
Copyright © 2013 by Chris Rylander

Library of Congress Cataloging-in-Publication Data
Rylander, Chris.
    The fourth stall. Part III / Chris Rylander. — 1st ed.
        p.    cm.
    Summary: "Mac and Vince have gotten out of their middle school
underworld crime business, but an upstart rival business and a run-in
with an old nemesis pull them back in"—Provided by publisher.
    ISBN 978-0-06-212006-9
    [1.    Business    enterprises—Fiction.    2.    Schools—Fiction.
3. Bullies—Fiction.]    I. Title.
PZ7.R98147Fq    2013                                    2012012717
[Fic]—dc23                                                        CIP
                                                                        AC

18  19  20    BRR    10  9  8  7  6  5  4
❖
First paperback edition, 2014

*For Steve Malk and Jordan Brown, real-life hit men*

# The Fourth Stall

## PART III

# Handcuffs or Body Bags

**S**imple.

My new favorite word. I never knew life for a kid could be so simple. Seventh grade had started just a month ago, and that's probably the one word that could best describe how my school year had gone so far: simple. Even the word itself had a kind of easiness to it, like it wanted you to say it over and over again.

Life was simple. And I liked it. I mean, I still couldn't figure out why other kids were always complaining all the time. School was a piece of cake when that was all that was on your plate and you didn't also run a huge business operation with multiple employees and a healthy cash flow.

This was my first school year since kindergarten that had started without my business up and running. I used to run my business with my business partner and best friend, Vince, in the East Wing boys' bathroom. Basically, if any kid in school had a problem, they knew they could come to me and I'd solve it for them. For a fee, of course. By the time sixth grade rolled around, we pretty much owned the school.

But at the end of last year, we had to end our business after coming clean and sacrificing its secrecy in order to save our school from this sadistic vice principal named Dr. George. At first, Vince and I had planned to shut our business down temporarily while the heat subsided.

But then near the end of summer, we both decided it was kind of nice to not have to worry about it for once. We could just focus on playing baseball, watching the Cubs, playing video games, going to movies, blowing up stuff with fireworks, etc. You know, doing normal kid stuff.

It was so nice that we decided just to shut the doors for good. Or, well, maybe not for good as in "forever," but at least for all of our seventh-grade year, and probably even longer. I mean, eventually our saved-up money, our Fund, would run dry and we'd maybe need to get some sort of business going again. And eventually kids would get tired of having to solve their own problems and they'd come begging for us to open up shop once again in the East Wing boys' bathroom, fourth stall from the high window.

One thing you can always count on: kids are going to find ways to get into trouble and are going to need someone to get them out of it.

Actually, several kids had come to me already to ask when we were reopening the business or to ask for help or advice. But I had turned them down each time. I was pretty determined to stay retired for now. The business used to be a lot simpler. It used to be just me and Vince and the problems kids brought to us. But last school year had been a nightmare. First we'd gotten involved in that mess with legendary crime boss Staples, and then a few months later a new principal had tried to take down the whole school. And our business had buried Vince and me alive right in the middle of both of those messes.

So, as much as it disappointed the kids who had come asking for help, and as much as I kind of did still want to help them out, I couldn't. I'd turned down every one of them. And they understood, for the most part, why I had to. They knew I couldn't open up business right away given all the attention we'd gotten saving our school last year.

Here's the thing, though: if you asked me, I might have said, even then, that I know deep down that it just wasn't going to be that easy to get out. There's this old trilogy of movies called *The Godfather*. They are some of my favorite movies because they kind of remind me of Vince and me. In fact, the first time I saw them, I had to double-check what year they had come out because I could have sworn the guys who wrote that movie had stolen some of my business tricks. Anyways, in the third movie, the main character says, "Just when I thought I was out, they pull me back in."

I just hoped it wasn't the same deal for me. Where the only way out was either in handcuffs or a body bag. Well, okay, my business probably wouldn't ever lead to anyone ending up in a body bag, but detention, suspension, or juvenile prison were all bad enough; and those were all definitely possible. Maybe worse than that if some of the juvie horror stories I'd heard were true.

Take this one kid Jack Knife who'd served a four-month stint upstate at the Estevan Juvenile Detention Center last summer. He was a changed kid when he got out but not in a good way. Kids hadn't always called him Jack Knife. No, back before he'd served his time, they used to just call him by his real name, Greg. Well, one day Greg accidently blew up his friend's dad's car while trying to prove that Twinkies are completely fireproof.

Anyways, the string of events that led to the car exploding are so crazy, you'd never believe me, but I was there and I saw it with my own two eyes. And by explode, I mean literally the car burst into a huge ball of fire. One of the tires got lodged right inside the middle of this old oak tree in his front yard. The fire chief had said it was a miracle that nobody got hurt. That kind of thing pretty much automatically earns you an extended stay at one of our state's fine juvenile correctional institutions.

Anyways, the point I'm trying to make is that Greg was a pretty good kid; he wasn't juvie type material. It was really just bad luck that he had happened to be experimenting with Twinkies, lighter fluid, and a blowtorch in the wrong place at the wrong time and caused an explosion so huge that to this day some kids say you can still feel the ground vibrating slightly where the car had been parked. But when Greg got back from juvie, he was a different person. He told me stories that I can't even bring myself to repeat. He said the only reason he'd survived was because he developed a signature move called the Jack Knife. It's pretty complicated and I'm not even too sure how it works, but let's just say at the end of it, the other kid looks like he just got run through a pasta maker, complete with ricotta cheese filling.

So that's what I was worried about. Becoming a human ravioli someday and getting sucked back into my business made it likely that this was going to be one of those things where the only way out was to go to juvie. And as much as having a cool nickname like Flint Cracker and a killer reputation to match sounded awesome, I didn't really want to go through what Jack Knife had told me he'd had to in order to earn them.

If only it could have been that simple.

It all started one day when I was walking home from school. I was walking because I was still grounded from using my bike due to the exposure of my business last year. I mean, I had helped take down an evil psychopath, so I had gotten off fairly easy, but that still didn't mean I escaped punishment altogether. Anyways, that's beside the point. The point is I was walking home one day and got a surprise visit from someone I'd thought I'd never see again. . . .

# Chapter 1

# That Was Easy

It was a pretty nice day, sunny and warm but not melt-your-face-and-start-your-hair-on-fire-if-you-stay-outside-longer-than-eleven-minutes hot like it could sometimes get in September. It was pleasantly warm on this particular day. Why is it that the worst things always seem to happen on the nicest days? Like when I'd almost gotten killed out at the Yard nearly a year earlier. The weather on that day had been almost perfect as well.

It was actually pretty funny that I was thinking about that whole thing at that very moment. I mean, not funny ha-ha but more funny-that-weird-coincidences-always-have-to-end-up-being-terrible.

So, anyways, I was walking home from school. Vince wasn't with me because he had to be home within fifteen minutes of school ending every day to watch his little sister. His mom had gotten a new job recently, which was cool because then she could, like, pay her bills again and stuff, but it also stunk because that meant he couldn't hang out until later in the day. So I'd been walking home from school alone this year. It wasn't so bad, really. I lived fairly close, and the trip always gave me time to think about how easy life was now. So far, every walk home had been entirely uneventful.

But on this particular day I heard a voice call out from behind me.

"Hey, Mac."

I didn't stop walking. Probably someone looking for help who hadn't understood that I wasn't in business anymore.

"Mac!" the voice said, louder this time. I was annoyed, and I didn't turn around. But I did stop walking.

"What?" I said.

"I need your help."

Just as I thought.

"I'm sorry," I said, as I had said so many times since school had started back up. "I'm not in that business anymore. I can't help you."

"I bet you'll make an exception for me."

The voice was closer now. Whoever it was had come out from wherever he'd been concealed, likely the bushes that lined the sidewalk. I could tell he was pretty much right behind me now. I could feel the cold of his enormous shadow engulf me. And that's when I realized who it was.

I'd know that shadow anywhere. I'd never forget it for the rest of my life. Which is why it was also impossible that I was seeing it; the owner of that shadow had skipped town shortly after I took him down. Everyone knew that. A circus family that had yard sales every other weekend lived in his house now.

Vince and I went there to check out the rummage sales every once in a while because they always had the craziest, funniest stuff. Like a purple feather vest designed to fit an elephant. Or a Poo Sling, a slingshot designed specifically to fling animal poop. And haggling with them was the best part. I wasn't as good of a negotiator as I expected. For my first purchase I managed to negotiate the price for a talking wig from seven dollars up to nine dollars. Yeah, I was that bad. But the wig was pretty sweet just the same. It could say only a few lines, but they were all awesome and insulting, such as, "Stop pulling on me, Scum Bucket" and "You make me look ugly, Crap Waffle."

Vince, however, was a master negotiator. He'd worked

the price of a car down to two bucks. Okay, so maybe it was only a model clown car and not a real one, but still, the original price had been twelve dollars.

But all this was beside the point. The point was that the circus family was there, living in the former house of the owner of this shadow. He'd left town. If he hadn't, we would have known about it. He was so legendary that someone would have seen him lurking about and said something. Right? Right?!

It didn't matter. All I could do now was turn around.

His smile hadn't changed much; it was still all teeth and menace. And his laser-beam stare could still melt a penny at a hundred yards. And he was still huge. And he still looked like he could crush a pair of fifth graders in each hand like soda cans.

"Hello, Mac," Staples said, smirking as always.

# Chapter 2

## Reformed and Retired

**S**taples still looked like Staples in that he still looked like he'd just gotten back from eating a nice leisurely lunch that had consisted of sick kids' puppies. But he also looked pretty different in some ways, too. For instance, instead of a shaved head, Staples now had short dark hair that was neatly combed. And instead of his usual tank top or T-shirt, he was wearing an untucked dress shirt and a skinny necktie and dark jeans. He looked like any other normal kid. Well, except for the evil smile and the dark eyes so black that even nighttime was afraid of them, that is.

In case you're not aware of who Staples is, which is unlikely considering he was a legend around these parts, he used to run a business kind of like mine. The only difference was that his business was dirty. He fixed things in his favor and rarely ever showed kids mercy. He'd beat you to death with your own arm if it somehow benefited him. And last year I'd gotten involved in an all-out war against him and his cronies. In the end, with help from my friends, we'd managed to take down his whole empire. Not long after that, we got word that he'd skipped town. And I had truly believed I would never see him again.

But I had been wrong.

Standing there now inside his impossibly large shadow, I tried to stand my ground. That's what I've learned about predators from the Discovery channel since my first run-in with Staples: Don't ever show your fear. Predators prey on the weak.

But he could see right through it, of course.

"Relax, Mac," he said. "If I was here to get revenge, you'd already be bleeding."

I managed to blurt out an awkward chuckle that only made Staples smile wider.

"And besides, I don't really want to get any of your blood on my shirt."

I took a deep breath and used every ounce of seventh grader I had to finally say something.

"So . . . what, um, do you want, then?"

Great job of not sounding weak and afraid.

"Well, I'm trying to turn my life around. 'Fly straight,' as my nerdy counselor likes to say," Staples said.

"Counselor?"

"Yeah, I've got this court-appointed counselor I go see once a week. You know, to help get me on my feet. I am eighteen with no legal guardian anymore, you know. I have to take care of myself."

"Court-appointed?" I asked lamely, not knowing what else to say.

"Yeah, I did a stint in juvie shortly after our, uh, *run-in* last year. Part of the deal my lawyer copped with the judge for me was that upon my release I'd have to start seeing this counselor. You know, to help make sure I don't ever find my way into real prison. But I don't even need him for that. I realized the error of my ways on my own."

I really had no idea what to say to this so I merely nodded. I thought if I even tried to speak I might accidentally yell, "Liar!" And then kick him in the shin and run. But that probably wouldn't play out to my advantage in the end, so I stayed quiet. Which was fine because Staples just kept talking.

"Yeah, anyway, he's a real dork, my counselor. But I guess he's trying to help me or whatever, so I try to stomach him and his dumb motivational sayings. You know what he actually says to me basically every time I see him?"

I shook my head.

"He says, 'Barry, *perception is reality*.' Can you believe that? He even says it all profoundly just like that. Like it's the most genius thing anyone has ever said. How lame is that?"

I had absolutely no idea what Staples was talking about now, so I just nodded dumbly. *Perception is reality?* What did that even mean?

Staples was still Staples after all, so of course he could read me like a book. Which meant he saw right through my pretending to understand what he was talking about. He laughed at me.

"Mac, just trust me when I say that if anyone ever uses that phrase, they're either an idiot or a liar. Or both. Because reality is what is real. Intent and actions are real. Perception is just that: a different and individual awareness of the reality that exists; that's why there are two separate words for it. And don't even get me started on the quantum physics angle, because then that phrase has a totally different meaning altogether, scientifically speaking, and last time I checked, my counselor definitely wasn't a quantum physicist."

"Umm . . ."

Staples laughed at my embarrassingly obvious lack of

comprehension. I felt uncomfortable thinking about just how smart he might actually be. I had always known he was smart, but his ferocity and criminal intent had perhaps always hidden the true extent of his intelligence.

"So what exactly do you need help with?" I asked, anxious to get away from this new intellectual version of Staples. Somehow, seeing him act even remotely nice and civil made me more nervous than when he was just a flat-out psychopath.

"I was getting to that," he said. "So I'm still trying to get custody of my sister. Right now she's living with foster parents and, according to what I've seen and read, some foster kids grow up to be just like my dad: drug-addicted, jobless, hairy, and for some reason they also always seem to collect weird crap, like used paper plates or hippopotamus figurines or, in my dad's case, orange highlighters."

"That's great," I said. "Well, I mean the part about you trying to do something good, not that foster kids sometimes end up like your dad. But, anyways, what could I even do to help you?"

Staples furrowed his mean eyebrows.

"What gives, man? Isn't that supposed to be your *thing*?" he practically shouted.

It was the first real glimpse he'd shown of what I knew he really was deep down. And I took a step back, deciding whether or not to either book it now or see if I couldn't distract him somehow first and then make my getaway.

"Well, yeah, but no, I mean, not anymore. I told you, I'm retired."

Staples grabbed the front of his forehead like he had a headache. I could tell he was trying to stay under control. It dawned on me how close I probably was to getting my left eye punched out the back of my head by this monster.

"Besides," I added quickly, "she doesn't even go to my school, does she? I mean, I kind of specialized in stuff at my school itself."

"No, she doesn't go to your school," he said flatly. "But I didn't either, did I? Yet you still somehow managed that problem okay, didn't you?"

He had a point. And it was pretty awkward to stand there listening to him talk about how I had taken him down the year before. I'd crumbled his independent empire and now here I was saying that I wasn't really capable of doing such things.

"Well, that's kind of why I'm retired—every time I get involved, it only seems to make things worse. It always ends badly for *someone*."

"Didn't I hear that you just saved your school recently? That doesn't sound like it ended badly to me," Staples said. "Sounds like you won, as usual."

"It's not about 'winning,' Staples; it was about solving problems and making money. And I was creating more problems than I was solving at the end, and also spending more money than I was making. Besides, I'm kind of in the same boat as you: I need to keep my nose clean. The Suits are kind of watching me, you know?"

As I said this, I nodded my head toward a car that was parked just down the street from us. Staples turned and looked. The plain gray sedan that had been parked there since Staples and I had started talking suddenly pulled out and peeled past us and down the street before turning a corner and heading out of sight.

As the car had driven past, the gleam off Mr. Dickerson's bald head had shined like a sniper's scope reflecting the sunlight.

Staples gave me a look.

"Yeah," I agreed, "it's insane. He's been following me every day after school. I mean, they're really paranoid. But it's hard to blame them. I've found out the hard way that businesses like mine usually lead only to trouble in the end. That's why I'm out."

Staples looked like he was about to protest, but in the end he just nodded.

"Don't you remember what you said to me the last time we spoke?" he asked.

"Yeah, I offered to help you get back on your feet . . . but that was a year ago. Things have changed."

"I guess they have," he said, sounding defeated. "Well, I suppose there's no point in me even telling you what exactly I wanted help with then, even though it was something that would have been right up your alley."

I was surprised at how easily he was giving up. I mean, he really could have forced me to help him if he'd wanted to. And now that he was giving up, I was kind of curious as to what exactly he thought I could do to help out his situation with his sister. But I knew better: if I started asking questions, then that'd be it; I'd be sucked right back into the life I was trying to avoid.

"I really am sorry, Staples. But you saw Dickerson. . . . The Suits are on me like glue stuck to the teeth of a second grader right now."

Staples didn't say anything else. He just nodded and turned to leave. And then without looking back, just like that, my old nightmare was gone. And I was still in one piece, which was why it was weird that I suddenly felt so horrible, guilty almost.

I know I said before that me getting pulled back into the Business all started with the visit from Staples. So okay, I admit it. Maybe Staples didn't exactly pull me back into my business directly, at least not that day, but the whole incident should have been the first sign that something was off.

If I'd seen the warning lights right then, maybe I could have avoided some of the insanity that followed. Stuff like swimming pools full of blood, guts, and body parts, and crazy third-grade Japanese assassins with precise, near-deadly hit man skills. The sort of stuff that happens only in terrible made-for-TV movies on Disney starring whatever teen pop-star happens to be popular that month. If I'd known what was going to happen, maybe I would have stolen a car, swung by Vince's place, and gotten us both the heck out of town before it could.

But I hadn't seen Staples's visit as that kind of sign. So instead I just walked home.

# Chapter 3

## The Death of Joe Blanton . . . Jokes

I called Vince the minute I walked in the door.

"Guess who paid me a visit today?" I said.

"Joe Blanton's mom?"

"Come on, Vince, I'm being serious."

"Me, too! I mean, I would pay you a visit, too, if you mailed me a bunch of snake skins stapled to a picture of my son."

I laughed in spite of myself. Of course I hadn't mailed Joe Blanton's mom anything, especially not a bunch of snake skins stapled to a picture of Joe Blanton. Last week I'd made a Joe Blanton joke so harsh that Vince had been joking about it ever since, about how I'd basically just desecrated the Blanton family name or something.

"Whatever, Vince. I'm kind of over Joe Blanton."

"How could you?" he nearly screeched. Joe Blanton was this pitcher we'd been cracking jokes about for the past year.

"Well, he only used to drive me crazy because he would dominate the Cubs even though he stinks, but I've come to terms with the fact that pretty much all pitchers dominate the Cubs. Even triple-A pitchers look like aces against them. I bet even Bobby Lovelace would no-hit them. It's not a Joe Blanton thing; it's a Cubs thing."

Bobby Lovelace was this kid who had pitched on our Little League team three years ago. He was epically bad. He's the only pitcher in history (at any level of baseball) never to record a single out in six starts. Why our coach ran him out there to start six games that season will forever be a mystery. Even Bobby himself didn't want to start any games after that first one, in which he allowed an unbelievable fourteen earned runs before finally getting the hook. All totaled he gave up sixty-three earned runs in six starts without getting an out. And, seriously, right now even he could probably dominate the Cubs' lineup.

Vince was quiet on the other end. It had been a particularly rough season for us this year. The Cubs were 57–81 so far, pretty much the laughingstock of the league, being that they had one of the top five highest payrolls. And just when we thought the curse couldn't get much worse, too.

"Yeah," Vince finally said, and left it at that.

"So, want to guess who it really was who asked me for help today?" I asked.

"Well, if I asked my grandma, she'd probably say it was Don Pablo, the little pirate monkey who likes to throw fish heads at birds down at the pier."

I gave him a moment to laugh at this (it *was* pretty funny) and then I dropped it on him.

"Staples."

There was a long silence. Vince usually processed information quickly, but I guessed this had really surprised him.

"That Staples?" he said after a while.

"How many kids named Staples do you know?"

"What did he want? How are you even still alive?"

I went over the exchange I'd had with Staples just thirty minutes before.

"Maybe you should have at least found out what specifically he wanted," Vince said at the end.

"I know, but if I got that far into it, then the next thing you know, we'd have found ourselves in the middle of another mess involving rabid wolves, zombie classmates, and a nuclear bomb with a faulty fuse. Right?"

"Yeah, I guess you're right," Vince said. "When exactly

did this business get so dangerous? I mean, remember the days when the hardest part was figuring out how to get kids answer keys to quizzes?"

"Right, I know," I said. "That's what has kept me so motivated to stay out, even with kids harassing me daily for help."

"Well, either way, I guess I'm glad you're still alive after running into Staples . . . even though it's so weird that he let it all go so easily. But at least now I get to stump you and crown myself champion of the Cubs universe once and for all."

"Bring it on," I said. Sometimes, a Cubs trivia challenge is the only thing that can take our minds off things like Staples returning to town.

"In honor of their miserable season this year, what are the most games the Cubs have ever lost in one season in franchise history?"

"Why would I want to sit around thinking about the worst seasons they've ever had? There are too many to count!"

"Exactly," Vince said smugly.

"But asking this means you've been thinking about it."

"Well, yeah," he said, sounding like he was starting to realize how depressing it was.

"The truth is," I said, "I've been wondering that, too, since they might beat that record this year. The answer is one hundred three losses, and they did it twice in the sixties."

"They suck," Vince said.

Then we both laughed. Of course we acted negatively and said stuff like that, but we both also knew that, come Spring Training next season, we'd naively believe, like we did every year, that they had a real shot to finally end the curse that season.

"You still coming over later to play video games?" I asked.

"Of course," he said, and then we hung up.

# Chapter 4

## Eeyore and Roberto

The next day three more kids came to me for help with their problems. Well, two came asking for help. The third came bearing an offer. But I'll get to that in a little bit.

The first kid approached Vince and me as we were walking to our homeroom. We were passing the hallway that we normally would have taken to my old office each morning. Both of our heads turned as we passed, thinking about the past six years spent in the East Wing boys' bathroom. Since the school year had begun, we'd pretty much avoided our old office in the East Wing. In fact, now that I was in seventh grade and in a different part of the school, I pretty much avoided the East

Wing altogether, like most kids usually did unless they were coming to see me for help. It was a good place for an office because there wasn't much of anything in that part of the school at all.

"Do you think the school has done anything with it?" Vince nodded toward our old offices.

"I don't know. Maybe. But what would they do, make it a museum? I mean, it's still just a nonfunctioning bathroom; there are not a lot of options."

"Well, my grandma always says, 'Your options are only as limited as the chocolate ice cream that you store inside of your skull. Give me some of that ice cream!' She shouts and then tries to twist the top of my head open like it was some kind of jar."

I laughed. She'd actually tried to do this to me once, too. At first it had been terrifying—a crazy old lady trying to pop off the top of your head so she can eat the chocolate ice cream she thinks is inside of it—but she was so weak that after a few seconds it just kind of started to tickle, which made me laugh, and then his grandma laughed, too, and then she forgot what she'd even been trying to do in the first place.

Just then I noticed another kid had started walking next to Vince and me.

"Hey, Nick," I said, nodding to the newcomer.

"Mac, Vince. I got to talk to you guys," Nick said.

"What's up?" I asked, even though I knew what was coming.

He shrugged and made one of his faces. "Well, first, I lost my iPhone. And my bike frame got scratched. Plus, I heard from this one kid that the Dolphins might trade away their star linebacker for a measly fourth-round pick, but they'll probably be terrible anyway, so I guess it doesn't matter. Then I broke Brandon Decker's new glasses by accident when I tripped in the lunchroom and spilled my food all over the kids at his table. Oh, and my pet turtle died yesterday."

Now, you might hear this and feel bad for Nick. Like, how much tragedy could befall a kid in a week, right? But that's the thing about Nick: this was pretty normal for him. He hadn't earned the nickname Eeyore for nothing. In fact, he seemed to be more positive than usual today. Whenever you asked him how he was doing, he'd launch into an answer so depressing, a black cloud would form around your head and you'd feel like you were drowning in bad news. Plus, he always talked really slowly and sadly, just like Eeyore, the donkey from those old *Winnie the Pooh* cartoons. I kind of always imagined Nick to have a trombone player following him around playing depressing and dubious baritones. Eeyore used to be a pretty frequent customer of mine, but in recent years he'd stopped coming because, no matter what I did to fix his problems, he always came up with new ones caused by my solutions. I'd have been offended by anybody else complaining so much about my solutions, but everybody knew that's just how he was.

"Rough week," I said.

Eeyore shrugged slowly. Cue a few blats from a trombone.

"It's been better than last week," he said. "Last week I had a splinter in my finger all week that got infected. Then I had a toothache and my mom's car had a flat tire on the way home from the dentist and we had to walk like three miles, which gave me blisters on both feet. I went outside the next day and got some gravel stuck in my shoe, and I hate taking off my shoes because one time I took them off for like two minutes and someone stole one of them. So then the gravel got stuck in my blister and it hurt all day. The blisters just now are starting to go away, but I ruined my favorite socks the day they popped. Plus, my favorite TV show got canceled. Then at dinner on Friday my sister sneezed on my food, and I'm pretty sure she got me sick. And I lost my favorite lucky penny." *Blaaaah-Ruuump.*

Vince stifled a laugh. That was really the only way to react to Eeyore: humor. If you let him get to you, you ran the risk of slipping into a depression-induced coma from which you'd probably awaken thirty years later to find a strange world where the Cubs have moved to Wyoming (yuck!) and a racist house cat named Neil has been elected president.

"Anyway," Eeyore continued, "can you help me?"

I took a deep breath in preparation for my usual speech about being retired, but he must have been able to tell what I was going to say because he interrupted before I could even get started.

"Please, Mac? I'll pay you in advance for everything. I mean, thinking about all these problems is giving me a headache. Plus, my eyes already hurt from this lighting," Eeyore said while trying to shield his eyes with his hand. "Where do they get such bright lights? Don't they know we'll all get cancer from standing under these things? Not to mention the eyestrain, I mean, my uncle lost vision in one eye from staring at his computer screen too long every day at work. Now he just sits at home all day in the dark and drinks gross tea, which is tea that is too cold to be hot tea and too warm to be iced tea. And his car rolled into the river behind his house last week, too." *Blaaaah-Ruuump.*

He knew my weak spot: payment up front. But before I could open my mouth, Vince jabbed me with his elbow as we walked—a painful reminder of how these things had spiraled out of control in the first place: not knowing when to say no.

"Look, I'm sorry, Eeyore, but I can't help. It's just too dangerous for me now. If I help one kid out, then I'll have to help others and then, well . . ."

He nodded in defeat. "Yeah, I figured you'd say no. Would this change your mind?" He took out a crumpled wad of cash and held it out to me. "Like I said: payment up front."

I looked at the cash in his outstretched hand. There must have been at least fifty bucks there. That was a lot of dough. Then I glanced at Vince. He was also staring at the money, his eyes glistening like glazed hams.

"I've been saving all summer. I need your help," Eeyore said. "Please."

I looked at Vince again; this time he was looking back. He shook his head slightly. I knew he was right.

"What time is it? We have to get to homeroom," I said, picking up the pace, hoping Eeyore would get the hint.

"I don't know," Eeyore said. "I try not to look at clocks much; you know they say that staring at clocks too often can cause cancer, right? Plus, I read this article online that said keeping track of time too frequently can lead to stroke, heart disease, and early onset diabetes and can also accelerate the development of Alzheimer's disease. Not only that, but I had this kitty clock once that fell off the wall and smashed my Xbox into seven pieces. And that was on my birthday, which is also the same day John Lennon died." *Blaaaah-Ruuump.*

"Yeah, well, what doesn't cause cancer these days?" I joked. I know it's not cool to joke about something as horrible as cancer. My grandma had died of cancer a few years ago, so I really do know how crappy it can be. But it was all I could do to keep from slipping into a depression coma

"I know, exactly. Life is a war zone, Mac," Eeyore said somberly.

But he'd gotten the hint because then he just nodded in defeat and veered off away from us toward his own homeroom classroom. I looked at Vince, and we both sighed and shook our heads as we headed into our homeroom. Homeroom was the only class we had together that year.

The second kid to ask me for help that day did so almost as soon as we took our seats in homeroom. I hoped eventually kids would start giving up because there's only so much a guy can take.

Vince and I sat down next to each other, and then the kid in front of us turned around so violently, his desk almost tipped over.

"Mac, Vince, I need your guys' help!" he practically shouted.

It was JJ Molina. He was known to overreact to stuff. Melodramatic, I thought, is what I heard an eighth grader call him once. I didn't know exactly what that meant, though; whenever I heard that word, for some reason all I could think about was snooty actors wearing skinny jeans and drinking Mello Yellow. But just the same the word did seem pretty fitting for JJ just from the sound of it. He was always worked up about something.

"Calm down, JJ," I said, "you're going to hurt somebody."

"Right," he said, taking a deep breath. "I need your help."

"I'm retired; you know that by now, right?"

"I know, Mac, but you gotta help me!"

His eyes were wide and panicked and had a crazy look to them like the kind I imagined mine would have if, say, Vince ever went missing. I thought for sure I might see JJ grind his teeth down to the gums right in front of me.

"Okay, I probably can't help you, but at least tell me what's wrong," I said, knowing I should have stayed stronger. I just couldn't help it: after years of always being there, it just wasn't that easy to walk away cold turkey.

"It's Justin Johnson. He ripped me off!"

"Figures," I said.

Justin was always up to no good. Stealing stuff from kids, fighting, vandalizing the boys' bathrooms, crop dusting the hallway, etc., etc. At one point last year he was in charge of Staples's business dealings at our school. So I'd had my fair share of run-ins with him.

"He followed me home after school yesterday, and once I was like a block from the school, he jumped me!" JJ said. "He stole my mint-condition, *autographed*, 1955 Topps Roberto Clemente rookie card!"

I shook my head. That was some card. Roberto was one of the few non-Cub players who I really loved and respected. I knew that card was pretty valuable: in mint condition (which is pretty rare for a card so old), it could be worth anywhere from $1500 to $5000 or more without his signature. But an autographed version? The sky was the limit.

JJ nodded. "It's my prized possession. He's the best baseball player ever to come from my parents' country, you know?"

"Yeah, I know . . . but the thing is—" I started, but JJ didn't let me finish.

"Please, Mac, can you help me get it back? That card was a gift from my father; it was his when he was a kid. I'll never be able to afford another one," he said. "Plus, there aren't that many that exist that are autographed."

He was actually fighting tears now. JJ was a pretty tough kid, so it must have hurt pretty bad to lose that card if he was this close to crying in a school class-room. I mean, any time after second grade, crying in school was social suicide.

"Look, I wish I could help. I really, really do," I said. "But I just can't get involved. The Suits are all over me the way it is. If I try anything, I'll get expelled or sus-pended before I could help anyway. Have you thought about going to the Suits yourself? I mean, they could probably do something for you."

It made me feel violently ill to suggest to somebody to go to the Suits for help with a problem. But what else was I supposed to do? I felt so bad for JJ, but there was nothing I could do to help. I was retired. And I was being watched closely. Where did that leave me? I had no choice, right? Right?

JJ nodded slowly. But his head stayed low. He avoided looking at me or Vince again, and then without saying anything else, he slowly turned around in his desk and flopped his head down onto the hard surface.

As I watched JJ Molina cry quietly at his desk, all I could think was: What have I become?

"It was the right thing to do," Vince whispered, prac-tically reading my mind like he sometimes seemed like he could.

"I know; it's just hard to say no. I mean, who else is going to help him? Or Eeyore, or any of them?"

Vince shrugged. "It's like my grandma says, 'When you need help, just start screaming as loud as you can and people will come running . . . just don't let them steal your scrambled eggs. You must always guard your eggs at all costs.'"

I laughed in spite of the fact that I was serious about what I'd said. I really did wonder how the kids at our school were going to handle suddenly having no one to help them with their problems. It's like they say in cheesy movies: sometimes you don't know what you really have until it's gone.

# Chapter 5

## Rookie of the Year

The third kid who tracked us down that day, the one who had an offer for us, found us during lunchtime. Or, well, I guess he didn't find us so much as he had us found.

Vince and I were hanging out near the west goal post of the practice football field, waiting for kids to finish their lunches so we could get a short football game going before the start of fifth-hour classes.

"Remember that time we tried to pull a *Rookie of the Year*?" Vince asked as we played catch with the football.

I laughed as I remembered that incident. We had been in fourth grade; it was the beginning of the baseball season. Vince and I had watched this old movie called

*Rookie of the Year* because it was about the Cubs. We watched everything we could find that mentioned the Cubs. Anyways, in this movie this kid hurts his arm and it heals weirdly and gives him a cannon for a throwing arm. So naturally he joins the Chicago Cubs baseball team to help save their season and end the curse. And because it's a movie, and not real, it works out in the end. This thirteen-year-old kid ends the Cubs curse and they win the World Series. Overall the movie was just okay, but it gave Vince and me an idea. Probably the best idea we'd ever had up to that point.

I mean, Vince was already a good pitcher, right? So really we thought our plan was pretty genius. And maybe it could have worked if he had separated his throwing shoulder in the fall instead of his other shoulder. But I guess having Vince jump off the roof of the school wasn't really that good of a plan in the first place. We had never really considered that he wouldn't be able to control entirely what body part he landed on. But it's hard to blame us; we were only fourth graders, after all. And being a Cubs fan can kind of blind you to logic sometimes. We were just that desperate to somehow break the curse.

Of course I can't even begin to explain why even after the first failed attempt we still thought the plan could work and tried again. The second time we had Vince jump off a Jet Ski going at full speed and try to land as awkwardly on his throwing arm as possible. After that fracture finally healed and he couldn't throw any harder than before, we finally decided to let the idea go.

"That *was* pretty awesome," I said.

Vince faked being upset. "Yeah, for you maybe. You're not the one who had to suffer through two arm injuries!"

"It's not like you didn't love all the attention you got from girls because of that sling. They were just lining up to do your homework for you and help carry your books and stuff."

Vince grinned and shrugged. "Whatever. It still wasn't as much fun as it would have been to pitch for the Cubs."

"Speaking of the Cubs," I said, "I bet I've got you."

"You wish."

"Who was the last Cub to be inducted into the Hall of Fame?"

Vince scoffed. "Well, sorry, but I'm not an idiot and thus know that the answer is in fact Ron Santo."

"Yeah, I know that was an easy one. I just thought I would honor the fact that those morons finally let him in like he deserved to be."

Vince nodded, and we shared a few seconds of silence in honor of good old Ron.

Then suddenly two hands came out of nowhere, grabbed my arms, and pinned them to my sides. I saw

Vince hit the ground as someone pushed him.

"Hey!" I said.

My assailant let me go, and I turned around as Vince climbed to his feet next to me. He seemed unhurt— thankfully we were on grass and not gravel or pavement. We'd been ambushed, basically. Had we still been in practice, we might have seen it coming, but with the simple life of not having a business came less paranoia. My head wasn't always on a swivel like it used to be.

"What gives?" Vince said.

"Jimmy needs to talk to you," one of our attackers said, pointing at me.

It was Mitch. One of Staples's former lackeys, a guy who had plenty of reason to dislike Vince and me. The other kid was this brutish eighth grader named Lloyd Ahler, a real gorilla of a kid who I didn't know much about since he had been new here last year. I had been too busy last year to get to know most of the new kids.

Mitch wasn't too big and tough, but he did have a year on us. And Lloyd looked like he could have driven Vince into the ground with a single overhanded swing of his giant mallet of a hand. I figured fighting back or running wouldn't end well, especially since they didn't seem to be here to fight.

"Jimmy who?" I asked. "Jimmy 'the Dutch Axe' Pierson?"

"No, not Jimmy 'the Dutch Axe,' you idiot," Mitch scoffed.

I didn't see how me not knowing who he meant made me an idiot since there were like seven Jimmys at this school. But I didn't argue the point. I just stared at him.

"Jimmy who, then?" Vince asked.

"Jimmy Two-Tone, duh," Mitch said.

"Look, I don't know a Jimmy Two-Tone," I said, and started to turn away.

Lloyd "Gorilla" Ahler grabbed my arm with what I could only assume was a robot hand since it squeezed so hard.

"Yeah, well, he knows you, apparently," Mitch said. "And he has requested a meeting with you."

"Me? Why?" I asked, even though I knew better. Clearly it was just another kid in need of help. A kid so desperate that he'd hired two eighth-grade goons to come and make me hear his request.

"I'll ask the questions here, okay?" Mitch said.

I shrugged and nodded. Then a long silence followed. It was kind of uncomfortable.

"Well, are you going to ask me a question, then?" I said finally.

"Oh, well, I guess . . ." Mitch started. "I guess I don't have any questions, exactly. Look, stop messing around. I said Jimmy wants to talk to you!"

I looked at Vince, who merely shrugged.

"Okay," I said.

"Okay, then," said Mitch, clearly not quite used to this sort of thing. There was a definite difference between recreational bullying and bullying for pay, being a strongman, and he hadn't quite worked out the subtleties just yet.

Lloyd was holding my arm a little harder than was necessary considering I'd agreed to come with willingly, but I wasn't about to insult this walking lump of hair and muscle that called itself a kid named Lloyd. And so we started back toward the school in silence.

# Chapter 6

## Jimmy Two-Tone

Lloyd and Mitch escorted Vince and me to the cafeteria. Vince and I normally avoided the place, even now that we didn't have a business to tend to during the lunch period. For one thing the lunchroom smelled like rotten potatoes and cheap grandma perfume. Also, the lunchroom was like a bully's playground. Operating my business had gotten me on the bad sides of a lot of bullies over the years, due to the number of kids who came to me for protection or payback. So it was usually just safer for Vince and me to avoid the lunchroom altogether unless it was necessary, like last year when we had to come down here to investigate a case for Jonah the health freak.

Mitch and Lloyd led us toward a lone table wedged in the back corner of the lunchroom by the row of long windows. There was only one kid at the table, and he sat there with a plate full of something fluorescent purple in front of him. He gazed out the window while taking a bite of the purple stuff that looked to be more radioactive than edible.

We all stopped in front of him. He was a mostly normal-looking kid. Maybe sixth grade or so. I didn't recognize him, which meant he was likely new. At the start of every school year there were at least four or five new kids that came along with it.

Lloyd let go of my arm and nudged me forward. I rubbed the spot where his cyborglike paw had been clamped.

"What's this, guy?" Jimmy Two-Tone said. "Did you rough them up?"

Lloyd shrugged and then grinned. Mitch smirked.

Jimmy scowled at them.

"What gives, dudes?" Jimmy said. "I didn't say to do that! They're my guests. Apologize to them. Now."

"That's all right. It's not a big deal . . . ," I said.

"No, no, no, friend, it *is* a big deal. That's no way for someone of your reputation to be treated. No way at all," Jimmy said. "So what are you waiting for, morons? Apologize!"

Lloyd rubbed his neck and then muttered, "Sorry."

"Yeah, man," Mitch said.

"To both of them," Jimmy said.

They repeated their sorrowless apologies to Vince, and then Jimmy waved his hand and they both sulked off to a nearby table.

"Sorry about that, buddies," Jimmy said with a smile. "Have a seat."

He shoveled another spoonful of bright purple chunks into his mouth as we sat. He must have seen me looking at the plate trying to figure out what it was.

"Oh, I'm being rude. Want some pickled beets?" he slid the tray toward us.

I shook my head without trying to make a face at the horrible vinegar smell wafting toward me.

"No thanks," Vince said.

Now that I was closer, I saw why his nickname was Jimmy Two-Tone. He had two different-colored eyes. One was light blue, so light it was almost white, and the other eye was dark brown. It made him look about as creepy as any kid I'd ever seen.

"So, you, uh, wanted to see me?" I said.

"Yeah," he said before swallowing another huge bite of beets. "Jimmy heard about what you did for this school, guy. Pretty good stuff, pal."

"Yeah?" I said, feeling pretty impressed that he'd heard of me.

"That's right, dude. Jimmy heard that you guys ran the best business this side of the Missouri. That you helped out lots of kids. Jimmy also been hearing stuff about you retiring now. Is that right, friends?"

Was he referring to himself by his own name instead of saying "I" and "me" like a normal person? What gives with this kid? Either way, though, he seemed nice enough. Besides, it's not like he was the only weirdo going to school here. This place was packed with odd-ball characters. It's part of why I loved it so much.

"You heard right," I said.

Jimmy grinned then nodded. "Why? Why you guys retiring? I mean, lots of profits still to be made here, right, bros?"

I nodded. Today had shown me that much, maybe more so than any other day so far this school year. There were still plenty of kids with plenty of problems to be solved. Which meant there was a lot of money still sitting on the table.

"Well, if you heard all the rumors about us, then you must know why," Vince said.

Jimmy grinned again and shrugged. "Well, yeah, sure Jimmy hears stuff. But he'd rather hear it from the goat's mouth himself before he believes it. I mean, you dudes gotta know you can't believe everything you hear, right, guy?"

Goat's mouth? I glanced at Vince and we exchanged a brief look. I tried to figure out if Jimmy was eccentrically brilliant or just another regular old weirdo.

"After a series of events last year, the heat was on. We didn't have any choice, not if we didn't want to be expelled. The Suits are still on us." I nodded my head back and to the left.

Principal Dickerson was standing against the far wall pretending not to be staring at us. He'd followed us here. He kept an eye on Vince and me almost every lunch period.

"Yeah, that's quite some problem you got there, friend," Jimmy said. "So the Suits are watching you, making sure that you aren't up to any funny business. But that means they can't be paying as much attention to the rest of us, right? It's a simple numbers game. There are more of us to monitor than they have the manpower for."

"Numbers don't lie," Vince agreed. I think he suddenly felt way more comfortable knowing we were sitting across from another numbers guy. Jimmy was strange, yeah, but he was also clearly pretty sharp.

"What are you getting at?" I asked.

"What about if someone new came along? Someone who the Suits would have no reason to suspect of
wrongdoing. Someone with pretty good business savvy
and a squeaky clean record. Someone who could step
in and fill the void, solve kids' problems, fix everything
that got broken last year. What would you say to that,
friends?" Jimmy took his last bite of beets and then
leaned back and stared at us as he chewed, his multi-
colored eyes seeming to play tricks on my brain.

I looked at Vince. He looked back. Neither of us knew
what to make of it. I don't think either of us had ever
considered handing off the reins of our business to
someone else. Especially not to a new kid who we had
just met.

I think Jimmy could read what I was thinking
because suddenly he leaned forward and spoke in a
low voice.

"Okay, Jimmy doesn't think he's going to come in
and replace you, just like that. Mac and Vince probably
can't ever be replaced, right, bros? But Jimmy also don't
need you to show him the ropes or anything, because
he knows that would be too risky with Dickerson on
your tail the way he is. The thing is Jimmy ran a pretty
similar operation back at his old school, so he knows
what he's doing."

I nodded for him to continue.

"Right, well, what Jimmy is suggesting is that he runs your business for you. Jimmy will take over that sweet office I heard you had and maybe some of your old contacts could become Jimmy's contacts, right? I mean, kids still got problems they need solved. And you can't help them anymore. But that doesn't mean that Jimmy can't help them. And here's the best part, guy: Jimmy will cut you in. It's your operation; after all, you did the hard part already. It's like a bike: it's a lot harder to build a bike than it is to ride one. So Jimmy cuts you in for ten percent of the profits, and if any trouble shows up from the Suits, Jimmy will be the one taking the heat. It's win-win-win. Kids still get their help, you still get paid, and it's risk free."

"But why cut us in at all? You could have just come in and started your own business either way," I said.

Jimmy looked offended. "Come on, guy! Don't be like that. Jimmy would never undercut another business-man on his own turf. What you take Jimmy for, some two-bit hood? It's the right thing to do, friends. Jimmy needs your blessings."

"Can we have a few minutes to talk about it?" I asked.

"Of course, dudes," Jimmy said, and then slid his chair loudly over to the table where Lloyd and Mitch were playing some sort of game that involved them repeatedly smacking each others' wrists.

"What do you think?" Vince said once Jimmy was clear.

"I don't know. I mean, first of all, can we trust him?"

Vince shook his head. We both knew it was a good question. I didn't like the idea of handing over my business to someone who might dirty its reputation. Then again, Jimmy, despite being weird, did seem to have things mostly in order. And he had gone through the trouble of making sure we were on board.

I pointed this out to Vince and he agreed. Besides, if Jimmy was untrustworthy, then he'd probably start his own business either way. So we might as well start out on his good side regardless. Especially if there was some mostly risk-free money to be made along the way.

"I mean, really," I added, "making this deal is sort of our way of really getting out, right? If we hand over the business to someone else, then that's it. We're done except for the small franchise fee we'll be getting. This is what we wanted. . . ."

Vince nodded slowly. "Yeah, and then also all of these kids' problems can get fixed, too. We won't get harassed all day and have to feel so guilty all the time. Mac, this kid just made us an offer we can't refuse."

"So we're saying we'll give him the okay, then? It all

makes sense, but it just feels so . . . weird."

"It's like my grandma says, 'Nugget.'"

I waited. Vince just looked at me evenly.

"That's it? 'Nugget'?"

"Yeah, some days she just wanders around the house saying 'nugget' over and over again. It's weird."

I grinned and shook my head and then signaled to Jimmy.

He rejoined us at the table. "So what's the deal, bros?"

"Make it fifteen percent of the profits and you got yourself a deal," Vince said before I could respond.

Jimmy looked at each of us with his best poker face. Then a smile slowly spread across it. "All right, it's a deal, dudes!"

He held out his hand and we all shook on it. Then we got down to the business of discussing the intricacies of the East Wing boys' bathroom, the fourth stall from the high window, and most important, the method of payment for our cut of the green stuff.

# Chapter 7

# TINSTAAFL

I'll fast-forward a few weeks here to spare you on the boring stuff. That's right, for two whole weeks nothing bad or crazy had happened to us. In fact, boring is about the only way I can describe the first two weeks following our deal with Jimmy. Or normal. Either word works.

But I'm not complaining. I mean, I loved it. Now that I was truly out, life couldn't have been better. Kids had even stopped coming to me to plead for help within days of our arrangement with Jimmy.

It didn't take long for the word to spread about Jimmy reopening my business. And apparently he hadn't been joking around: he was pretty good at it. The kids I'd talked to all said he was fast, fair, and efficient. I even heard he got JJ Molina his Roberto Clemente rookie card back. Some kids seemed to think Jimmy might even be better at running the business than I had been. Which was annoying. . . . I mean, it's like Jimmy said, building the bike is harder than riding it. But, whatever. If they were all happy, then I was happy. Especially since Jimmy was cutting Vince and me in on all of his profits just like he'd promised. He was making the cash drops right on schedule, every Monday and Thursday like clockwork.

We had a pretty good system for the drops, too. One of Jimmy's guys would package our cut and wrap it in sealed plastic, like in a Ziploc sandwich bag. Then with the cash hidden in his shirt he would go into the North Wing boys' bathroom at 12:02, just after lunch had started. He'd stash the money in the bottom of the trash can underneath wads of used paper towels. A place where no sane, unsuspecting kid would ever randomly decide to stick an arm into.

Then at 12:05 Fred would enter the bathroom and retrieve the bag. He'd enter a stall and remove the cash. He'd take his cut out, which was pretty minimal, and then conceal the rest of the cash in his backpack. Then sometime after lunch and before afternoon recess he'd walk past my locker and slip the cash in through the vents.

That might seem complicated. And, yeah, it was. But we just couldn't be too careful with Dickerson on our tail the way he had been. Vince and I learned over the years from watching a lot of mobster movies like *The Godfather* that dirty money had to be laundered to conceal where it came from. We wanted our link to the current business to be as weak as possible.

Anyways, on that third cash-drop Monday when I opened my locker, my knees almost buckled. There was a small lake of cash at the bottom of my locker. Seriously, I practically needed a boat just to fish out my gym shoes.

Later that day after school when I showed Vince and we counted the money, we could hardly believe it. There was more than one hundred dollars, all totaled.

"Mac, there's no way this is fifteen percent. It has to be more!" Vince said. "I mean, if this is actually fifteen percent, then Jimmy just beat our all-time four-day profits record by two hundred and ninety-eight dollars!"

"That's not just beating our record, Vince. That's obliterating it."

"How is that even possible? He'd have to see like ninety customers per day. There's just not enough time for that to be possible. The numbers don't add up, Mac. And numbers don't lie. It's like the TINSTAAFL axiom in action right before our eyes."

My social studies teacher had taught us about that on the first day of class this year: TINSTAAFL (pronounced "tin-staw-full"). It means, "There Is No Such Thing As A Free Lunch." Which basically means if a deal seems too good to be true, then it probably is.

All money going out in business, in life, in the universe, eventually needs to equal or reconcile with all money coming in. If we were making this much money, then who was losing out?

"He must just charge more money than we did?" I suggested. "Also, he might offer more of an express type service. You know, faster results but less personal attention and treatment. He goes for volume.

Vince nodded. "I guess."

And so we added the money to our Funds, and didn't talk about it again that week. Especially not after Thursday. Because that was when Vince and I realized Jimmy's business practices were the least of our problems.

# Chapter 8

# Big Brother Is Watching You

**V**ince called me around four o'clock that Thursday. This wasn't too unusual, as we talked to each other or hung out pretty much every single day. But I could tell right away that something was different about this call.

"What's up? Did you call to try pointlessly to challenge my vast Cubs knowledge?" I said.

"Mac! You gotta get over here!"

"What? Why?"

"You're never going to guess what happened. . . . This is bad, this is so bad," he said.

"Hey, it can't be worse than the way the Cubs season has gone. I mean . . ."

"Mac, listen to me!" he yelled. "That's nothing

compared to this. Now get over here. You're never going to believe this unless you see it."

Then I heard a deep voice in the background say something and laugh. Then I heard what sounded like a small scuffle, and Vince said something I couldn't make out, but I could tell that he was even angrier and more upset than he had been just seconds before.

"I gotta go, so get over here," Vince said, and then the line went dead.

I was still grounded from my bike technically, but I took it anyway. I didn't think I could survive the length of time it would take me to walk to Vince's. I had no idea if he was in trouble, what kind of danger he might be in, what was waiting for me when I'd get there. But the one thing I knew was that I was going to get there as soon as I could.

My parents had stashed my bike on some shelving that ran across the rafters of the garage. It was a place they thought I couldn't get to, but they were wrong. I climbed up using my dad's workbench as a ladder. Then I crawled over to where my bike was and slowly lowered it as close to the ground as possible.

It was still a pretty good drop, but I had no other choice, and I let go of the bike. It clattered to the garage floor loudly but landed in one piece. Then I set off for Vince's.

Everything looked okay from the outside of his place. I mean, his trailer wasn't engulfed in flames or anything. The lights were on; everything was relatively quiet aside from the sound of cars driving on nearby roads and kids playing in the trailer park playground behind Vince's mobile home.

I knocked, and Vince answered a split second later.

"What's going on?" I demanded.

"Come on," Vince said, motioning for me to follow him to his room. "You'll need to see for yourself."

Vince didn't have a gaping head wound or broken bones poking through skin or anything. So I followed him back to his bedroom, a place where I'd spent many hours hanging out, playing video games, watching the Cubs, and even having an epic fight or two.

That's when I saw him.

"Hey, the other one! Perfect!" Staples jumped up from Vince's desk chair and punched my arm playfully.

By "playfully," I mean it felt like someone had just taken a sledgehammer to my bicep. I grabbed my arm and tried to laugh off the punch, but it was hard even to stay upright, it hurt so much. I saw Vince tenderly holding his own arm, and I kind of wondered how many "playful" punches he'd gotten already.

Staples was still dressed well, like he had been when he visited me a few weeks earlier. Except this time, there was that glint of sadistic glee in his eyes that I kind of had never wanted to see again.

"How's it going, *Christian*?" Staples asked, and then laughed.

What exactly was going on here? I knew Vince's mom would be getting home from work any minute. Surely she'd put an end to whatever sort of sick torture Staples had in mind for us. I looked at Vince to ask what Staples was doing here. At first he just squirmed uncomfortably. Finally, he spoke.

"He's my new big brother," Vince said.

"What?" I shouted. "I thought his dad got sent away or is in jail or something! Plus, how could your mom possibly be into that guy? No offense, Staples."

Staples didn't seem offended. He just kept grinning at me.

"No, not like my real big brother. He's my *Big Brother*, through that program for kids with no dads. My mom thought that that whole thing with us getting caught last year with our business and all the bad stuff we did was because I don't have a 'positive male role model' or whatever. So she signed me up!"

"We're all going to be good buddies now!" Staples said with delight. Clearly he still loved making me uncomfortable.

"Why are you in the program?" I asked him. "And

why would they take you?"

"Hey, now," Staples said. "Let's try not to insult me too much, Mac, right? Anyway, it's like I told you a few weeks ago. I'm trying to get custody of my sister. Participating in the Big Brother program is one of the best ways to score points with the courts. And they took me because, technically, my whole criminal record was wiped clean when I turned eighteen. That and I think they're kind of desperate for volunteers, especially in this neighborhood."

He had a point: there wasn't exactly an abundance of model fathers in this part of town.

"Makes sense, I guess," I said.

"Yeah, it does."

Staples doled out another round of arm punches for Vince and me. Getting hit in that exact same spot hurt so much, I thought I would go blind in one eye.

"So you're just going to be hanging around us a lot more, then, is that it?" I asked.

"That's right. I've got this so-many-hours-per-week schedule that I have to fulfill. Man, what a lucky draw for me to get Vince," Staples said, leaning against Vince's bedpost. "Right? In all seriousness, I think I might have a thing or two to teach you guys."

Vince and I looked at each other awkwardly. I had a lot I wanted to talk to him about, but it was weird to discuss anything with Staples standing right there.

"So are you two still retired, then?" Staples asked.

"Sort of," I said. We proceeded to explain to Staples the deal we'd made a few weeks ago with Jimmy Two-Tone.

"Let me tell you something, Mac," Staples said after thinking it over for a minute. "You can't ever truly get out. Didn't you know that when you started this business? Once you choose this life, you're in it forever, or at least until you're dead. I'm sure this seems like the perfect setup right now, but don't forget, there's a business at your school, and in the end, it's all going to be tied to you. Getting out means cutting all ties completely, even leaving a part of yourself behind. There's no such thing as halfway out in this business. Believe me, I know."

His words carried an ominous and dark weight to them, like thick, heavy rain clouds ready to dump tons of water onto an unsuspecting town. But at the time, with things going so well, they weren't what I wanted to hear.

"Look, Staples," I said. "Things have changed a bit since the last time you were in business. We've got this under control. In fact, if you still need help help getting your sister back, you might consider paying Jimmy a visit."

Staples shook his head.

"No, I've changed my mind since I last talked to you. To accomplish anything meaningful it needs to be on the level. I need to do this the right way for once. I just can't risk losing my sister again. Getting her back and taking care of her is all I've got left, and the last thing I want to do is blow it by getting involved in some two-bit middle school crime ring."

I had never heard Staples be so serious about anything. Still, I didn't buy it. He had to have an angle he was playing. People like Staples don't just change that drastically overnight. The question was what exactly did he have up his sleeve?

"Hey, it's like my grandma sometimes says," said Vince, finally chiming in. "'If it ain't on the level, then you'd better hope that the penguin starts puking up strawberry-banana gravy.'"

I'd never heard that one before, and so in spite of the tense mood I couldn't help but laugh. Then Vince laughed, too, and I swore I even saw Staples crack a smile as he pulled his phone out of his pocket and started typing on it.

"All right," I said. "I better go home before my parents notice that my bike is gone. If they haven't already."

"How about the ultimate question before you go?" Vince said.

"Yeah, if by 'ultimate,' you mean 'insanely easy,'" I said.

"Cubs pitching great Charlie Root supposedly once said, 'I gave my life to baseball, and I'll only be remembered for something that never happened.' What was he referring to?"

I froze. I couldn't believe it, but he actually had me. I opened and closed my mouth a few times somehow hoping the right answer would just come out on its own. I mean, I was vaguely familiar with the name Charlie Root because I knew he was up there with Mordecai Brown among Cubs pitching records, but he never got the same recognition as old Three-Finger Brown. I felt like the answer should have been obvious and that I'd be kicking myself once I found out what it was. I was just about to offer up a random guess and accept my defeat when Staples spoke.

"He was the pitcher during Babe Ruth's called shot at Wrigley in game three of the 1932 World Series," he said.

Vince and I both turned and stared at him in shock.

"What? I'm a Yankees fan, remember? By the way, who, ah, won that World Series again?" he taunted.

Obviously the Yankees had won. Neither Vince nor I gave in to his goading with a response. Vince was probably upset that Staples had bailed me out, but at the time, I think he was more in awe of his baseball knowledge than anything else.

"You're right," he finally said. "But to be fair Ruth never actually called the shot; everybody knows that's an old baseball legend. It's like Charlie Root also said later, 'Ruth did not point at the fence before he swung. If he had made a gesture like that, well, anybody who knows me knows that I would have put one in his ear and knocked him on his ass.'"

"Yeah, you would say that, sore loser. You Cubs fans are all the same. You just whine about everything and make excuses and always blame everything bad that happens to the Cubs on everybody else but the Cubs. Whether he pointed or not, no one can deny he hit a home run or that Gehrig hit one right after that and the Yankees went on to win the Series that year. Right?"

Staples shrugged an empty and insincere apology of sorts and went back to typing on his phone.

Man, who ever would have guessed that I'd be pulled out of the clutches of Cubs trivia defeat by Staples? Or that for the first time in my life I'd be happy to be in the same room as him, even if it was for only a few seconds?

# Chapter 9

## Abby

Having Staples around as a third wheel for the next several days was complicated, and by that I mean it was terrifying, nerve-racking, difficult, painful (my arm felt like it could fall off at any moment), surreal, and—okay, I kind of admit it—at times even kind of cool. I know that sounds crazy, but being seen out in public acting like we were friends with a legend, an eighteen-year-old legend at that *and* one who attracted attention from lots of cute older girls, was pretty awesome. I can't lie about that part of it.

Plus, he was pretty funny once you got past all the arm-punching and how much he made fun of Vince and me for pretty much everything we did or wore or said.

And he was sort of like the sadistic version of Vince's grandma in that he kept giving us advice on business, girls, life, all that stuff. Except instead of giving crazy and illogical advice like Vince's grandma, Staples's was actually helpful. Even if it was sometimes a little demented.

Some of the things he'd said to us over the past few weeks included such treasures as:

"You're only as tough as your actions show you are. That means you won't intimidate anyone if all you do is talk tough. People will see right through that. You need to bust some heads. That's what will get you respect. A great man once said, 'Speak softly and carry a big stick.' Which is great, even if my advice would instead be 'Speak loudly and carry a big stick.'"

"If you get into a fight and you're both still standing at the end, then you're both losers."

"Despite what people say, money *can* buy you happiness. Like, I'm not talking about eternal happiness or anything, but more on a day-to-day moment-by-moment basis. Let's say right now I was to give you two hundred dollars with absolutely no strings attached. Well then, would you or would you not be happier than you had been just moments before? And that extra happiness would probably last you a good day or maybe even two. See, it's simple logic: money can buy happiness even if it's only temporary. Besides, isn't all happiness tempo-rary by definition?"

"Stealing stuff is easy. It's knowing what is actually worth the risk of stealing that's difficult."

"Girls love to talk about themselves. If you like a girl, just ask her lots of questions about herself, you'll get a date in no time."

"Never hesitate in anything you do, ever. That's like a cardinal rule for all life on earth. In a duel between two sharks, two tigers, whatever, whichever side hesitates when the time to attack comes will end up dead."

"Don't trust anybody completely. Ever."

"If you ever see a clown somewhere other than at a circus, rodeo, or party, then either run away or kill it immediately."

"Keep a roll of quarters gripped tightly in each hand if you ever get into a fist-fight. Trust me, they will help."

Anyways, the Saturday after he first showed up in Vince's trailer, Staples wanted to take Vince and me to the go-kart track as a part of his Big Brother thing. At first, I didn't want to go, but I couldn't just bail on Vince like that.

I was technically grounded, of course, but when I explained the Big Brother situation to my mom and about how Vince wanted me with since it was awkward to hang out with Staples on his own, she understood and let me go.

When Staples showed up to get me with Vince already riding shotgun, I felt kind of dumb for being such a wuss about the whole thing. For one thing Staples apparently didn't have that old red muscle car with racing stripes anymore. He showed up in a regular-looking, blue Toyota sedan. Also, he and Vince were actually laughing about something when they pulled into my driveway, as if they were actually having a good time. Go figure.

I got in the backseat behind Vince.

"I need to make a stop before we go to the tracks," Staples said as he backed out of my driveway.

Vince turned and glanced at me, indicating that he had no idea what was up. I shifted in my seat. I saw Staples glance at me through the rearview mirror.

"Don't worry. We're not going to a drug deal or anything. I just want to stop by and see my sister for a few minutes. Her foster parents don't like me very much, so I can only see her briefly and when she's not home."

"I thought you were doing everything on the level," I said. "Sneaking around her foster parents for covert meetings doesn't exactly sound aboveboard."

"Hey, I just said they don't like me. It's not illegal for me to hang out with my sister for a little bit if I want. I just do it when they're not around because there's no point in me causing any unnecessary trouble right now."

"How often do you visit?" Vince asked.

"I don't know. As much as I can, I guess. Maybe a couple of times a month. I'm just . . . I'm trying to not overdo it until I work everything out with the courts as far as me getting custody."

"So, why did you trade in the sports car for this thing?" I said, trying to change the subject.

"It's a Toyota, Mac. There are billions of them. Look," Staples pointed out the window at another blue Toyota parked on the street. "Same car. I figured it would look better for me to drive an 'everyman' car instead of my dad's old attention-getter. You know that flashy sports cars get pulled over by cops way more than regular cars, right? Statistically. Plus, insurance on that thing was insanely expensive. So, once I lost my business . . ."

He trailed off, but shot me a pretty nasty glance through the rearview mirror. I sometimes forgot what the consequences were of me taking down his business.

An awkward silence followed as we headed out of town and in the direction of Thief Valley, a smaller town that was just about fifteen miles away. Then out of nowhere Staples started talking again.

"My sister's so freaking smart," he said. "Smarter than me. And you guys look like morons compared to her, no offense."

"Uh, none taken?" I said.

I realized that I'd never heard Staples talk this way before. Every time he talked about his sister, all traces of his sarcasm were gone. Instead he looked . . . I don't know, like a little kid thinking about his first trip to Disneyland or something. It was weird and it kind of made me uncomfortable for some reason.

"I mean," Staples continued, "if it weren't for her, I probably would be in prison or worse. But she needs me. I'd give anything to be able to hold her hand again the way I used to when I walked her to the playground when she was in kindergarten."

He moved a hand from the steering wheel to his face.

Before I could stop myself, I asked, "Are you crying?"

"So what if I am?" Staples said. Then he reached back and slugged me right above my knee. I grabbed my leg and winced and rocked back in my seat. It felt like I'd just got run over by a freight train loaded to capacity with African elephants.

Staples reached over and got Vince on the arm, too, for good measure, I guessed. We didn't say anything for the last several minutes of the drive. It was safer that way.

We finally pulled up in front of Thief Valley Elementary. It was a Saturday, but apparently a lot of kids rode their bikes to the playground on Saturdays. That's sort of how things worked in smaller towns, you made do with what you had. And in towns like Thief Valley, the schoolyard playground was likely the most fun place to hang out in grade school, even on weekends. There were twenty or so kids playing on the swings and monkey bars and the rest of the stuff. And there was even a small game of football going on behind the playground. Staples parked on the street right by the playground.

"Let's go," he said.

"Us, too?" I said.

"Yeah, why not? Come on." He swung the door open and got out of the car.

Vince looked at me and shrugged before removing his seat belt and opening his door. I followed him, and we jogged to catch up with Staples as he walked toward the playground.

None of the kids was breaking away and running toward us, and I wondered what was going on. Finally, one girl who had been talking to some other kids behind the slide broke away and started walking toward us.

I barely recognized her from the picture I'd seen in Staples's office when we'd raided it last year. She was a lot older than in the picture. She was now in maybe third or fourth grade, and her hair was different.

"What are you doing here?" she said, stopping at the edge of the playground.

"Is it a crime that I want to say hi to my little sister?"

"Probably," she said. "Everything you do is a crime of some sort."

"Ooh, ouch," Staples said playfully, but I could tell he was hurt by the comment.

Vince and I exchanged looks. Staples's sister apparently wasn't quite as thrilled as he was about the idea of him getting custody. I wondered if she even knew at all that he was trying to.

"Anyway," Staples said, "these are Mac and Vince. They're my new pals. Mac, Vince: my sister, Abby."

Abby eyed Vince and me up and down, clearly not impressed.

"Why are they so young?" she said, even though we were at least several years older than she was. "Picking on kids your own age got too boring?"

Staples sighed and took a knee so he was closer to eye level with her. "Listen, I don't want to fight. I just came here to say hi. Mac and Vince and I are going to race go-karts, and I figured if you wanted to come—"

"Why would I want to do that? Besides, David and Linda would never let me."

I guessed that David and Linda were her foster parents. The whole thing was getting uncomfortable, and I glanced up at some of the other kids on the playground. This monster of a kid was terrorizing two other kids by the swings. From his face he looked no older than fifth grade, but the rest of him . . . Well, he was like an industrial barge with skin, limbs, and a face. Or a woolly mammoth. He was holding one of the kids upside down by his ankle, and he had the other one pinned to the ground under his foot. It was horrifying. I looked at Vince and caught his attention, then nodded toward where the beast was flinging around little kids like he was fluffing pillows.

I made a move toward them. There was no way I could stand there and let that happen. But Abby held out her arm and stopped me.

"You don't want to do that," she said.

"But—" I started.

"Trust me. You shouldn't get involved with him. He's pretty powerful and stuff. It's best just to stay out of it. Those two kids will be okay. Besides, they kind of started it."

I wasn't so sure, but I nodded and stepped back. Mostly because, in all honesty, I really didn't want any part of getting into an altercation with a fourteen-foot-tall grizzly bear posing as a grade-school kid.

"David and Linda," Staples said, and then shook his head.

"They're not *that* bad," Abby said.

I'd been interviewing and reading people long enough

to know how empty her words were. It was as easy to read on her face as if she'd written it right across her forehead: they were that bad.

"You sure you don't want to come?" Staples asked.

"Definitely *not* with you."

"I'm going to make everything up to you," Staples said, getting back to his feet. "I promise."

"Yeah, just like Dad said he would, too. Right. Besides, I don't need you to. In case you haven't noticed, I can take care of myself just fine." Abby backed away a few steps and then turned and ran back to her group of friends behind the slide.

Vince and I looked at each other uncomfortably. Were we, like, supposed to say something to Staples? Should I pat him on the shoulder? Of course the answer was no. That'd be like poking an already angry tiger in the ribs.

"All right, guys, let's go," Staples said, and then started trudging back to the car.

# Chapter 10

## Who Cut the Lemonade?

None of us talked much on the way to the race tracks. And we especially didn't talk about Abby. We mostly just passed the time by talking about the current baseball season and how bad the Cubs sucked that year, which Staples found hilarious, of course. But then, he was a spoiled Yankees fan, so who cares what he thinks. At least Vince and I like a cool, authentic team, and once the Cubs finally break the curse, it will be a *real* championship, not a purchased one. Today's Yankees fans don't know what it's like to *earn* anything, the real way. But whatever, back to the story.

I have to admit that racing go-karts with Vince and Staples was pretty fun. Afterward we were all in pretty good moods. Which is why I thought during the drive back to our houses that it might finally be safe to bring up what had happened in Thief Valley. It seemed like the only time Staples was truly genuine was when his sister was involved or connected in some way to the conversation or events.

"So, TV Elementary is a pretty rough scene, huh?" I said.

"Yeah, did you see that yeti pummeling those kids?" Vince said, taking my lead.

I waited nervously to see how Staples would react. I shifted my leg back as far as I could. It couldn't handle another shot today. There was already a deep purple bruise developing where Staples had gotten me the first time.

But he didn't reach back again. This time he just nodded calmly.

"Yeah, I went there back in the day," he said. "It's always been tough. Kids there like to . . . well, assert themselves a little more than usual, I guess. That's part of why I want to get her out of there. I mean, going to that school *and* living with those foster parents . . . that's two strikes against her having a good childhood and turning out happy as an adult."

I nodded.

"Makes sense," Vince agreed.

"If I get custody of her, then she can go to your school, since I live in your district. You guys like it there, right?"

I laughed.

Staples gave me a confused look in the rearview.

"Things are great there," Vince assured him. "Mac's laughing because we turned ourselves in, exposed our business last year—something we'd never thought we'd do—all because of how much kids love that school. So, yeah, I think Abby would be much better off there than Thief Valley."

Staples nodded but didn't say anything else for a while.

"Well, if I told my grandma about this, she'd probably say, 'Just don't ever trust a person with three hands. It may seem neat that they have three hands and all, but I ain't never met a mutie that had a conscience. I also ain't never met one that didn't own a lobster for a pet; those muties sure love their lobsters. But don't ever trust a person that gives a name to a lobster neither.'"

"Mutie?" I managed to ask while laughing so hard I almost kicked the back of Vince's seat.

"Yeah, it's what she calls mutants . . . which to her are basically anybody who doesn't look like they could have starred in *The Brady Bunch*. Like, at the mall this one time we saw this kid with a Mohawk, not a fake one like tools wear but a real one, like two-foot-high spikes and the sides shaved to bare skin. She just kept screaming, 'Mutie! Mutie! Someone check its pockets to see if it's got papers!' I don't even know what she meant by that, but I was too busy laughing to ask her."

"Man, your grandma is the best," I said through more laughter.

Even Staples was laughing now, too.

Then suddenly he hit the brakes and swerved the car to the curb, nearly taking out a mailbox.

"Hey, you guys want some lemonade?" he said, pointing to a few younger kids with a lemonade stand on the street corner ahead of us. "Come on. This is exactly the sort of thing that Big Brothers were invented for."

We all got out of the car and approached a small table sitting on the sidewalk in front of a house. A couple of younger kids selling lemonade sat behind it. While it was kind of weird how suddenly Staples had pulled over for this, I couldn't deny that on a scorching, early-fall day like today some ice-cold lemonade would be pretty awesome.

Two small girls and one boy sat behind the table. They were probably third graders, give or take a year. They had a handmade cardboard sign taped to the front of the table that read: "Ice Cold Lemon-Aid Only $3 Bucks!! A Bargan! Clearance!!!" Three dollars was definitely a little steep for this neighborhood but whatever.

They'd figure out how proper pricing could maximize their profit eventually.

Staples ordered three glasses. They poured iceless lemonade into three tiny Dixie cups, and then one of the girls said, "Nine dollars, dude."

Staples grinned and handed her a ten-dollar bill. "Keep the change."

We downed our too-small drinks. And I almost had to spit mine out. Not only was it not ice-cold, but it was warm. And it was terrible. Given its color and consistency and temperature, I couldn't be positive that what we'd just drunk wasn't actually some kid's pee with lemon flavoring.

"Yuck!" Vince said while grimacing.

Staples also spit out his nasty lemonade, but he didn't get upset like Vince and I had. Instead, he just seemed mildly amused by this whole exchange.

"Is this cut?" I asked them. "With water or something? You can't charge a premium price for a product that's been cut with water. This tastes like lemon carpet cleaner!"

"We can do whatever we want!" one of the little brats said back.

"But why would you do this?" Vince asked, trying a different approach. "Don't you want people to come back?"

"They'll come back because every other stand around here serves the same stuff," the little boy said. "They're all owned by the same guy, so people got no other choice."

"And what about how warm it is? If you advertise ice-cold drinks, then they need to be at least kind of cold," I said.

"Hey, boss's orders," one of the girls said. "Boss says ice is too expensive."

"Who owns these stands?" Vince asked. "Who is your boss?"

"Jimmy Two-Tone, duh," she said while rolling her eyes at our apparent stupidity.

Vince and I looked at each other. Why would Jimmy Two-Tone cut corners on something as simple as a lemonade stand? Especially when, up to this point, he seemed to be proving himself as a more than capable businessman. He was doing just fine without opening up a reputation-tarnishing lemonade scam.

Staples smirked at us. "Still so sure that your deal with him was a good idea?"

Instead of answering, I threw the Dixie cup at the little trash can next to the table. It bounced off the rim and landed in the yard behind the kids. Staples laughed while I stomped around and picked it up and then placed it into the garbage can.

I wasn't sure exactly what all this meant, but I intended to find out.

The next morning at school I tried to track down Jimmy to ask him what was going on. But he was nowhere to be found. I checked the East Wing hallway, but the closed-for-repairs sign was up.

So at lunch Vince and I went to find Ears. Ears was my main source of information. He was the biggest gossip in the school and heard everything. If you wanted to know what kind of cereal the kid that sat next to you in science class puked into a cute girl's lap last year during homeroom one day, Ears could tell you that he had definitely heard that it was Corn Bran with sugar on it.

So Vince and I found Ears behind the old metal slide on the playground to ask him what he'd been hearing about Jimmy. Ears always hung out by the old metal slide, and he was always there with three or four of the more popular girls at school. I had no idea what they talked about all the time, but something told me I didn't even want to know.

I tapped him on the shoulder right as he was laughing and making fun of how "that girl over there looks like a linebacker in that sweater."

Ears turned around. Then his eyes widened and he grinned.

"Hey, Mac, Vince. I thought you guys were retired?"

I shrugged, made a face, and then noticeably looked at the pack of girls he had been talking to.

"Oh, right," he said. "One second."

He turned back and said something mostly inaudible to the girls, and they all started giggling before wandering over to the monkey bars.

"Better?" Ears asked me.

"Sorry, Ears, it's hard to kick old habits," I said. "Anyways, we are retired. I just wanted to ask you a few questions . . . for, ah, mostly personal reasons."

His smile grew, making his already giant ears stick out even more. He kind of looked like a coffee mug with a handle on each side. Then he held out his hand, palm up. I looked at it, then back at his face.

"Pay the man," I said to Vince.

Vince sighed and took out a five from his wallet and gave it to Ears.

"Sorry," Ears said, "but, you know, it's hard to kick old habits."

"Yeah, yeah," I said. "All right, I'm just wondering what you've heard about Jimmy Two-Tone's business? You know, how are things going? Are kids mostly satisfied? Is he delivering on his promises? Solving problems in a timely fashion? That kind of stuff."

Ears nodded slowly. "Yeah, things have been good

mostly. I haven't heard too many complaints. I mean, word is that a couple of whiners have been complaining that his hired help can be a little mean sometimes, but what do you expect from guys like Justin and Mitch and Lloyd, right?".

"He hired those guys on a permanent basis?" I said, suddenly worried that I'd handed my business over to Staples Junior.

"No, no, I mean, they're jerks all right, but word is they've been pretty well behaved, actually. For them, I mean. From what I hear Jimmy runs a pretty tight ship. He's fast. And good. Like, he always seems to be prepared no matter what. I've actually been thinking maybe he's a little too good, a little too prepared, if you know what I mean."

"Well, no, I don't, actually," I said.

Ears grimaced like I was asking him to run a mile instead of explain himself.

"Well, remember last week when eleven bikes had their tires slashed?"

I nodded.

"Yeah, our friend Fred was one of the owners," Vince said.

"Well, several kids whose parents wouldn't or couldn't buy them new tires came to Jimmy for help, and he just happened to have a bunch of extra bike tires on hand."

Vince and I glanced at each other. That was pretty odd, no doubt.

"Maybe he anticipated he'd need them after the first few slashings," I suggested.

"Yeah, *maybe*," Ears said. "But still, you have to admit it was a little convenient."

"What else?" I asked.

"Then there's our team's last football game . . ."

"Yeah," Vince said. "What about it?"

"Well, not many people heard about this, since it never became an issue, but fans of the other team stole our team's shoelaces right before game time. The reason no one heard about it wasn't because the school had emergency laces on hand. What I heard is that Jimmy just *happened* to have twenty-five sets of brand-new shoelaces with him. The equipment manager bought them off him right then and there. Either he's psychic, or something fishy's going on."

I started to respond but then stopped. What was there to say? Assuming all of that was true, it certainly didn't look good. Was it possible Jimmy was creating all the problems himself to drum up extra business? That was about as crooked as it gets.

Vince must have been thinking the same thing. "Any

rumor out there that Mitch or Justin or Lloyd or maybe even Jimmy himself was involved in the bike slashing or the stolen shoelaces?" he asked.

"Yeah, some kids actually thought that might be the case, but my most trusted sources tell me that the four of them pretty much all have alibis for most of these things. That's what makes it so weird how prepared he is. Anyway, you guys have your five bucks' worth."

Ears walked toward the monkey bars and his snarky popular girlfriends.

Vince and I looked at each other.

"This is getting complicated," I said.

Vince could only nod in response.

# Chapter 1

# Watch Out for Sponges

**L**ater that day at afternoon recess we did something we thought we'd never do again: we went to the East Wing boys' bathroom.

We got there as quickly as we could, but there was already a line of customers. Mitch and Lloyd stood outside the door doing the job that Joe had done for me during the past few years.

Vince and I didn't want to risk waiting in line. We'd already had to pay this bully Little Paul to cause a scene out in the playground to distract Dickerson so we could get down there undetected. But that would only keep the principal busy for so long.

We went to the front of the line.

"No cutting," Lloyd said, and took a step toward us.

"We really need to see Jimmy. It's important," I said, holding out my hand, a five-dollar bill tucked into the palm.

He slapped my hand away. "I said no cutting!"

Man, didn't this kid know how to take a bribe? I was about to just give him the five dollars in plain sight along with written instructions that this was, in fact, a bribe, but Vince stepped in first.

"Don't you remember who this is?" Vince said.

Lloyd shrugged. Mitch knew, of course, but he didn't say anything.

"This is Mac, the guy who handed this business to Jimmy. What do you think Jimmy will say when we tell him later that his gorilla doorman didn't let in the founder and godfather of his business?" Vince said.

Lloyd and Mitch looked at each other. Lloyd looked to be helplessly lost in his cavernous brain. But Mitch scowled and then stepped aside.

"Go ahead," he said. "We haven't let in the first customer yet, so Jimmy is free. But hurry up; we've got a lot of people to see today."

I glanced at the line; it had almost doubled in just the few minutes since we'd gotten there. Mitch wasn't kidding.

Justin Johnston greeted us as we entered. He smiled,

but not in a Hey-How-Are-You sort of way but more in an I'm-Going-to-Enjoy-Smashing-Your-Face-In sort of way. I guessed he must have still been pretty upset about what we'd done to him last year when he had been working for Staples.

"Hey, guys, great to see you," he said sarcastically.

I just gave him a head nod in return. Then I noticed what they'd done to my formerly clean, professional, intentionally nondescript office. They'd desecrated it with a giant *Scarface* poster. Now, a lot of guys think *Scarface* is like the be-all and end-all in gangster movies. The coolest thing ever. But we true gangster-movie fans know that *Scarface* is like a stupid ant compared to the giant scorpions that are the *Godfather* movies. Not to mention *Goodfellas*, *Casino*, *The Departed*, and *Miller's Crossing*.

*Scarface* is like *The Godfather*'s ugly and stupid third cousin who the whole family is embarrassed about. I mean, okay, sure, on its own it's an *okay* movie. But the way everybody treats it as the Holy Grail makes me sick. Never, ever be friends with a dude with a *Scarface* poster.

"Like it?" Justin asked.

I nodded, trying to stay polite. It would be best to keep this civil, I had a feeling.

Then he led us into the fourth stall from the high

window. The very stall that used to be my office. The setup was similar to mine; there was a small desk inside and two chairs across from each other. The main difference, I supposed, was that this time I would be sitting on the other side of the desk.

"Hey, guys, how's it going?" Jimmy asked.

"Well, okay," I said. "How are things here? I heard you've been working a pretty tight ship?"

Jimmy grinned and nodded. "The payments have been pretty big, haven't they?"

"Sure," I said, "but then, it's not too hard to make money when you're selling a cheap and shoddy product."

He raised his eyebrows. "Huh?"

I told him about our experience at his lemonade stand that weekend. About how we'd basically been swindled and that the kids said that's how all the stands were in the neighborhood.

"Jimmy had no idea! Jimmy subcontracted the stands, assuming someone else could be trusted to handle them. Business was a little busier than I'd expected at first so I had to divvy up some of the jobs; I had to outsource to other people. I swear Jimmy will make sure this doesn't happen again. Friends, that's a Jimmy Two-Tone Trademarked Pipe Lock Guarantee."

He seemed to be genuinely surprised and even a little

angry about the shoddy lemonade stand being connected to his name.

"Okay, but what about the fact that you're always conveniently prepared for any number of random problems? You have to admit, it seems a little suspicious."

"Hey, guys, Jimmy just likes to be prepared. It's part of why I'm so good at this. Jimmy *anticipates* things. The best businessmen see things before they happen. You dudes should know that better than anybody."

It was a good argument, but I still didn't buy it. Something seemed off about all of this. I could tell Vince was thinking the same thing because right now would have been the perfect time for a grandma joke, but instead he just sat there silently.

"All right," I said. "But no more cut lemonade, right? I mean, my name is still attached to this business."

"Right, guy. Jimmy will take care of that. Don't worry about it. Now, if you don't mind, I've got a lot of customers to see."

Vince and I nodded and left the office.

On our way back to class we talked about what could be going on. It was really Jimmy's word against some random gossip, and even if the gossip was true, it was impossible to tell how much Jimmy was actually involved.

But before we could figure out what to do next, one of the hall monitors stopped us and told me Mr. Dickerson wanted to see me.

This couldn't be good.

The secretary told me to enter his office as soon as I got down there. I opened his huge wooden door, which seemed to be larger than the last time I had been here, for some reason, and stepped in, closing it behind me.

Mr. Dickerson was seated behind his desk, scowling. "Have a seat, Mr. Barrett," he said.

I sat across from him and tried to look as innocent as possible. I pretended I was a helpless puppy to try and get into character. I didn't think he was buying it.

"I thought we had ourselves an understanding," he said.

"We do. Why? What's this about?" I asked.

"You were spotted by a teacher down near the East Wing today," he said. "Want to explain what you were doing down there?

I took a moment to collect my thoughts before just wildly blurting out denials. I'd learned that getting instantly defensive usually didn't do anything but make things worse. For one, he'd said near the East Wing, not in the bathroom or even near the bathroom. Two, if he'd found out about other kids going down there, then this meeting would have been entirely different; it either wouldn't have existed or I'd already have been expelled. Which meant he didn't know much of anything. All he knew was that I had been in the area today.

"I was looking for Vince," I said.

"Why would he be down there?"

"Well, he wasn't. I only looked down that way because I couldn't find him anywhere else. Turns out, he was in the other bathroom. Got sick, apparently. I think it was the chicken we got served today. Are you sure they cook the chicken thoroughly?"

Dickerson actually growled then, low and slow like a mean dog just starting to get riled.

"That's enough of that," he said. "I'm tired of you kids making lunch jokes."

He then proceeded to lecture me for the better part of fifteen minutes about watching my mouth and knowing better than to go snooping around that area of school again, no matter what the reason.

"You narrowly avoided getting expelled for the last incident, Mr. Barrett," he said as he was winding down. "Your promise to stay away from that bathroom and stay out of trouble for your last two years at this school was a part of that deal."

I nodded and agreed, just like I had been doing the whole time.

He sighed and shook his shiny head. "I just don't get

it. . . . You could be such a good student. I don't get why you insist on causing so much trouble."

"I'm sorry, sir," I said again. It was pretty much the only thing he'd been allowing me to say. "I'll be more careful next time."

"Don't think I'm not onto you. There's something going on around here, and I have a feeling I know who's behind it. Know that the next time I see you anywhere near that hallway, or anything that even remotely resembles funny business goes down at this school, then you're outta here for good, young man! Expelled. You tell that to your friend, Vince, too. Got that? Now get to class."

As I walked slowly to my next class, I couldn't help but think of a Vince's-grandma quote he'd used earlier that summer. "Getting expelled ain't so bad. It's getting Sponged that you need to worry about. Sponges eat everything. I seen a sea sponge bite a man clean in half in his bathtub once."

If only that were true, then I wouldn't have been feeling so anxious about everything. I couldn't believe it had come to this again. Vince and me being out of the game had lasted all of a month. Whether or not Jimmy was telling the truth, something was definitely up, and now Dickerson was on my case even more than he had been. Staples was right—you're either in or you're out.

And, despite what we thought, everything we had tried to do, it's clear that we weren't out.

If I was going to figure this one out, the first thing I needed was more information. I decided right then that I would find Tyrell after school and put him on the case.

# Chapter 12

# The Talking Mailbox

I didn't get a chance to talk to Vince the rest of that school day. He and I didn't have a single class together that year other than homeroom right away in the morning, and that wasn't even a real class. So the only times we ever really saw each other during the day were at recesses and lunch. I was pretty sure the administration had rigged our schedules that way on purpose.

After school Vince had to rush home to babysit his little sister like usual, so I was left to track down Tyrell alone.

The trouble was I didn't really know where to look for Tyrell anymore. I started my search down at the new plastic playground, but he didn't seem to be there like he sometimes was. Then I checked the old playground on the top of the hill.

I was close to giving up when the blue mailbox on the corner right by the old playground talked to me.

"Mac!" it said.

I let out a yell and practically jumped up into the small tree next to me.

"I heard you've been looking for me," the mailbox said. "Do you have something to mail?"

"Huh?" I wondered if I'd accidentally eaten some of those mushrooms that grow behind the Shed down near the new playground that everyone said gave you weird visions.

"Just kidding, Mac," the mailbox said. "One second."

There was a clanking sound from within the large blue box. Then I heard metal sliding against metal, and a hand came out from the bottom of the mailbox, followed by an arm. Then Tyrell's face appeared and grinned at me. He squeezed the rest of himself out of the mailbox and replaced the false bottom.

"You cut that hole?" I asked, once again astounded at the kid's ingenuity.

Tyrell shrugged. "Yeah, I mean, technically it's a federal offense, probably even a felony, but normal laws don't really apply in the name of deep covert surveillance, you know."

I nodded even though I didn't really know at all. Tyrell was the best spy in the world, or at least in our school. Spies had a whole list of their own rules that I couldn't even pretend to understand fully.

"Besides, it'd be worth it even if I did get caught. You'd be amazed at how much great stuff you can witness from in there."

I laughed and then asked, "Did you really know I was looking for you?" I wasn't sure how that was possible since Vince and I had only decided earlier that afternoon to come talk to him.

"Of course," he said.

I waited for him to explain how he could have possibly known, but he simply left it at that and said nothing else. The kid was a marvel, and it usually was in your best interest not to even bother trying to ask how when it came to his methods. So I left it at that, too.

"So, what do you need, Mac? I thought you were retired?"

"I am," I said. "But just the same, I'm sure you've heard about Jimmy Two-Tone?"

Tyrell nodded slowly. "Yeah, he even tried to employ me once, but I passed. I mean, I don't do garbage assignments. He'd wanted me to spy on his sixteen-year-old neighbor or something."

"Ugh," I said.

"Yeah, Tyrell don't do no dirty, petty missions, guy," he said, doing an uncanny Jimmy Two-Tone impression. We both laughed.

"Yeah, well, anyways, I am retired and all, but it's hard to shake the feeling that something is up. I mean, on the surface, Jimmy Two-Tone seems to be a great businessman, but there are a few things that don't add up," I said. I then told him about everything Vince and I had seen and heard up to that point. "I mean, Ears said he heard Jimmy wasn't involved in creating the problems but . . ."

Tyrell made a face. I'd forgotten that he didn't really much care for Ears. Tyrell didn't trust anybody who operated solely on second- and third-hand information. He always said, "Mac, the only things you can really ever truly trust are what you see with your own eyes and what you hear with your own ears."

"Yeah, I know," I said. "I should have come to you in the first place. But I'm here now. Can you check it out for me?"

"Sure thing, Mac," Tyrell said.

"Thanks," I said as I shook his hand.

He pocketed the twenty-dollar bill that we'd exchanged during the handshake, his upfront fee, and then was gone. I had been standing right there, but I'm telling you I couldn't even have told you what direction he'd gone if I had been under oath and hooked up to a lie detector. He was that good. I shook my head in awe.

# Chapter 13

# Swimming Pool Bloodbath

For the next week Staples made us go to a ton of school-related events with him as a part of the Big Brother thing. He said they made him look extra good to his counselor and the court system and whatnot. And, man, there were even more school activities than I'd thought there were. Especially once you hit seventh grade.

It started the evening after I'd gone to Tyrell to investigate the circumstances surrounding Jimmy's business. We went to a seventh-grade orchestra recital. It was actually a pretty big event. The local news was there, and so were tons of parents and some random people who must have been pretty hard-core music aficionados. And of course Vince, Staples, and I. The orchestra played lame music and they weren't even that good, but then, as much as it scared me to admit it, Staples was kind of growing on me. And I really wanted to see him get his sister back. So we didn't put up too much of a fight.

The chairs were all set up onstage in the Olson Olson Theatre so that they created a rising tower of musicians. They had the first row seated on the lowest level and then the second row of chairs was about a foot higher and so on for four rows of chairs arranged in a half-circle.

We took three seats in the back of the theater and waited for the recital to begin.

"I can't believe we're here." Vince groaned.

Staples slugged him on the arm hard enough to make a lady a few rows in front turn around and shush us even though the concert hadn't even started yet and the stage was still empty. Vince rubbed his arm and made a face.

"What's wrong?" Staples whispered. "You guys afraid to get exposure to a little refined cultural arts? To experience some of the finest music our species has to offer?"

"I can't wait!" I said with as much sarcastic enthusiasm as I could muster.

Staples actually laughed. But then he slugged me on the arm, too. My already bruised and sore arm just pretty much felt numb, so it hurt only horribly bad instead of excruciatingly bad.

"This is going to look great on my report, though," Staples said, referring to his Big Brother events log report that was turned in to his Big Brother coordinator each week.

Vince and I exchanged glances.

"Oh, are you guys having a moment? Do you want me to leave you alone?" Staples asked, and then laughed again, this time louder. "You and the looks you're always giving each other."

The old lady in front of us turned around and shushed us again.

"Sorry, ma'am," Staples said politely.

Then the recital began. I think, anyway. I'd never actually been to an orchestra recital before. The conductor came up onstage, and everyone applauded robotically. The lights dimmed and kids started filing onstage. They all got in front of the chairs and held their instruments but remained standing. Then the conductor made a motion and most of the kids, except for those who needed to stand to play, sat down all at once.

That's when it happened.

Almost every single chair broke, and the whole setup came crashing down on top of itself into a big rumbling pile of kids, broken instruments, chairs, music stands, and even a few tears. It was chaos. The audience gasped; kids shouted. Staples snickered madly.

Vince and I looked at each other in shock. No way had that been an accident. Seventy chairs don't just break all at once.

Anyways, they were eventually able to get some of it set back up, but several instruments were damaged and some kids were hurt. Not seriously injured—there were no broken limbs that I could see—but they were still in too much pain to play. So the concert recital ended up being fairly short and disjointed. The whole thing had pretty much been ruined by the chair incident.

It was humiliating for our school; the next day the local newspaper printed a photo of the pile of kids, chairs, and instruments with a caption that read: LOCAL MIDDLE SCHOOL ORCHESTRA ATTEMPTS MASS STAGE DIVE AT CONCERT RECITAL.

Okay, so maybe that wasn't the most professional thing for them to have printed, but I had to admit it was a pretty funny headline.

Anyways, the whole thing left me in shock. I mean, chairs just don't break in unison for no reason, like I said before. To me, it was pretty obvious that it had been planned. At first I thought maybe it had been Staples, given how hard he'd laughed. But he genuinely looked surprised right after it'd happened. Plus, I didn't think he'd risk getting caught for a few cheap laughs with custody of his sister on the line.

On its own maybe the incident could be written off as some cruel practical joke that the marching band might have played on them. After all, our school marching band and orchestra had a pretty heated rivalry with each other for some insane reason. But the incident couldn't be viewed on its own. Because there were others.

The next night Staples made us go to this cake-decorating contest that took place in the school gym. That's right, a school-sponsored cake-decorating contest. That's one of the things that's sort of cool about my school: if you got enough kids and signatures gathered up, you could start pretty much any sort of after-school club you could think of.

Anyways, on that night, right before the judging phase of the contest, the school fire sprinklers in the gym all went off at the same time, drenching the entire audience (all twenty-five of us) and all of the cakes. They were all ruined, which was hard to watch. Well,

Staples snickered again, as you might expect, but I was pretty heartbroken for all of those kids who had worked so hard. One kid had even made this amazingly detailed 3-D Death Star cake complete with the trench and exhaust port and everything.

So maybe that incident was just random bad luck, right? Well, I tended to think that the timing of it was just too suspicious.

Then of course there was the swim meet that our school hosted later that week. Everybody showed up to find the pool filled with blood and guts and severed hands. It looked like a cannibal holocaust had occurred in there. Not even Staples was able to laugh at that.

Of course they later found out that it was just red dye and Karo syrup combined with hamburger meat and Halloween-marketed fake hands. Of course when we found out, we all agreed that at the very least it had been a pretty brilliant prank. Nonetheless, every time I tried to sleep that week, I could still hear the screams of those moms in attendance ringing in my ears. And the incident had made our school look pretty foolish. The meet had to be rescheduled, which annoyed all of the other schools involved.

Probably the worst one of all happened that Friday, when somebody spiked our football team's Gatorade with laxatives during a game. The second half was not pretty; you'll want to trust me on that. It got so bad that our team actually had to forfeit the game and take it as a loss even though we'd been winning 28–6. Of course, when the referee had made that call, he wasn't aware that the Gatorade had been spiked. He just thought the world was ending, like the rest of us.

That was the worst one in a lot of ways. For one, it counted as a loss for the team. And now they were 3–2 after two losses in two weeks. Our school and the whole town were pretty big into football and we expected to make the state tournament every year; we hadn't missed in decades. So this stuff couldn't keep happening.

And there was more, too, than just the stuff we'd witnessed ourselves. Some of the stories I'd heard kids telling around school involved:

A school assembly for grades one through five during which the whole room slowly started to reek like rotting milk until it got so bad that Dickerson had to postpone the end.

A school dance where somebody had coated the floor in vegetable oil just before it started, so pretty much everybody took several hard spills and one kid even sprained his elbow.

Three of the school science lab animals had been

dyed completely green, which was more funny than mean or bad, but still . . .

The school practice football field had a huge curse word cut into the grass so deeply one night that they basically had to strip all of the grass from the entire field to get rid of it. So we now have an all-dirt practice football field.

The school seemed once again to be falling apart. Only this time it was definitely due to direct and obvious acts of sabotage, as opposed to mysterious inner workings like what Dr. George had inflicted the year before. Plus, this time the end motive seemed merely to be to have fun at our expense, to ruin things and embarrass us. These were the sorts of things that Jimmy couldn't even possibly solve, which threw my theory right out the window that he was creating his own problems. There really didn't seem to be any grand master plan at work.

In fact, from what I'd been able to gather from kids talking at recess, Jimmy was falling behind. There was just too much for him to handle. We actually didn't even get our cut that Thursday. Our money drop was never made. And we couldn't even go ask him about it because I simply couldn't risk being seen near my old office again.

But anyways, the point was that it was pretty obvious that all of these incidents were related. The question was how. And why? Who had anything to gain from embarrassing the school and just wreaking general havoc?

# Chapter 14

## Mrs. King's Scarecrow

The Sunday after the most insane week I thought our school had probably ever had (yes, even more insane than when the SMARTs and everything had happened last year), Vince, Staples, and I were playing catch in the playground in Vince's trailer park. We were playing catch because Staples had said, "Having a catch is like the Super Bowl of Big Brother activities." But also, it was sort of nice to escape the recent insanity with some relatively mindless Sunday afternoon baseball.

Even if Staples kept trying to kill us.

We had a classic triangle going. I stood near the sandbox (the very same one that Vince and I had used as our first-ever office almost seven years ago), Vince stood about twenty yards away near his trailer, and Staples was standing about twenty yards from each of us in front of this creepy small scarecrow that Mrs. King had erected next to her small garden.

At first we had all laughed at the small but oddly ominous scarecrow, but as the afternoon went on, I saw Staples stealing small glances over his shoulder at it. It was making him nervous. It was kind of bizarre and hilarious to see Staples getting so jittery near an inanimate object, but at the same time it only made the scarecrow seem even creepier.

I maybe would have even laughed at him if he hadn't been trying to kill us, like I mentioned before. Every time he threw the ball to either Vince or me, he basically just rifled it as hard as he could. And he could throw pretty hard. I was guessing he even could have ended up playing at least college baseball if he hadn't gotten mixed up in the crime world as a kid and if his life had gone differently.

He laughed the first few times when it caught us off-guard and we had to duck or flinch as we caught the ball. But after a few times Vince and I were handling his fireballs with ease. That wasn't to say that my glove hand wasn't sore, but we were both good enough to at least make the catch every time without flinching.

Anyways, after a little bit we both started throwing back at him pretty hard ourselves. He handled our throws even better than we caught his, mostly because we couldn't throw nearly as hard as he could, not even Vince. All in all, it was the most tense and hostile game of catch that I'd ever participated in.

But then, Vince threw Staples one of his signature circle changeups. It's by far Vince's best pitch. It looks just like a slightly slower fastball until it gets to you and just falls off the table. Not many seventh graders can throw a pitch that breaks as much as that one does. So when it got to Staples, even if he had recognized it for something other than a fastball, he still likely would have missed it.

The ball sailed right under his glove, hit the fake trailer park playground grass, and bounced up and nailed the scarecrow right in the leg.

"Ow!" yelled the scarecrow.

I swear Staples must have jumped seven feet straight into the air. Then he turned and backpedaled away from the talking scarecrow so quickly he tripped and fell back onto his butt. Vince and I would have been laughing if we also weren't pretty spooked ourselves.

Then the scarecrow climbed down from its post and

took a step toward us. Its motionless burlap face with button eyes was fixed into a mouthless and dead stare. Staples was almost shaking, he looked so freaked out.

He climbed to his feet and took several steps back.

"If you come any closer, I'll tear your head off," Staples said, although it wasn't too effective of a threat since you could plainly hear the fear in his voice.

The scarecrow stopped walking and then reached up and tore its own face off.

"Please don't do that," the scarecrow said calmly.

But of course it wasn't actually a scarecrow. It was Tyrell.

"Who are you?" Staples demanded.

"He's a friend of ours," I said.

"Man, you guys have some weird friends," Staples said, shaking his head. "Who *does* that, seriously?"

I tried not to laugh. Tyrell, to his credit, just shrugged and smiled.

"What did you find out?" I asked. "Wait, let me guess. All of the sabotage of school events is somehow related to Jimmy after all, right?"

"It seems like it," Tyrell said.

"Ha-ha, see? Who needs you? We can figure things out for ourselves!" Vince joked. "It's like my grandma told me once, 'If you can see any of your own bones without a mirror, then everything is definitely not okay. Drink a milkshake immediately! And then call a banker!'"

We all laughed except for Staples. He stared at Vince and then said, "What the heck is wrong with your grandma?"

"She's a genius, that's all."

"Anyway," Tyrell said, "do you know *how* everything is related?"

"Hey, I gotta pay you for something," I said.

He nodded and then continued, "Well, turns out that I spotted some younger kids hanging around our school a lot. I saw some sneaking around right before all of the recent *incidents*, like the recital and the swimming pool bloodbath massacre. And these kids definitely don't go to our school, Mac."

This was all way too confusing. Why would another school be randomly sabotaging us?

"So how is that connected to Jimmy?" Vince asked. "I mean, he can't be paying them because those things are all causing him problems, too."

Tyrell shrugged. "Well, then this next part will really surprise you. I caught Jimmy making cash payments to some of the same kids who I saw sneaking around the pool right after the swimming-pool bloodbath."

I shook my head. This just didn't make sense.

"No way," I said.

"I've got video evidence if you really need to see it," Tyrell said.

Vince and I looked at each other. His head looked even more like it was about to explode than mine felt.

"So where are these kids from? Tell me you found out . . . ," I said.

Tyrell grinned and nodded, then furrowed his eyebrows, showing that even he didn't quite understand the *why* of what he was going to say next.

"They're from Thief Valley Elementary," he said.

I think all of us must have looked pretty funny just then with our mouths hanging open like idiots. After I collected myself, I handed Tyrell another ten-dollar bill.

"Well, thanks, Tyrell. Nice work as usual," I said.

"No problem," Tyrell said, and then seemingly vanished again. I mean, really, he just ducked behind some bushes, but once he was out of sight, it was like he had never been there at all.

Vince and I looked at each other.

"See?" Staples said. "That school is horrible. I've got to get my sister out of there before she gets involved in this crap."

"What now?" Vince asked me.

"I don't think this changes anything. I still say we

stay out of this. This is Jimmy's mess; he can dig our school out of it somehow."

"Really? You're going to let this spiral further and further out of control just like that?" Vince asked.

"I'm not letting anything happen! It's not my job to keep the whole school out of trouble," I said. "Besides, what can I do? Dickerson has been all over me. If I try anything, we'll get expelled, which won't help anybody."

I really believed what I was saying. To a point. On one hand, I knew that I was probably the only kid who could fix the problem before the sabotage got so bad that the football games would start getting played with samurai swords instead of a leather ball. But on the other, the Dickerson element was still the ultimate deciding factor. My hands were essentially tied.

I thought Vince realized the same thing because he sighed and then nodded in agreement.

"You can't just let this go!" Staples said loudly. "I knew that kids at Thief Valley are bad influences. You saw that kid who was basically bench-pressing two first graders the other day! You need to put an end to whatever sort of conflict there is between the two schools because I don't want Abby getting caught up in stuff like this. She's a good kid; I don't want her to end up like me. Plus, it's going to look really suspicious for me if she somehow ends up in the middle of some serious acts of school warfare right when I'm trying to get back into her life, you know?

"Besides, I *told* you there was no such thing as half-way out. You guys thought you could reap the rewards of the business without any of the consequences. Well, now you're right back where you started, looking down the business end of an expulsion. You see what I mean now, don't you?"

Staples had a point. He'd warned us something like this would happen and we hadn't listened.

He moved closer to me, so close that his shadow covered my face in darkness. His stare burned right through my head and probably set the grass behind me on fire. I tried to swallow, but my body didn't seem to be functioning anymore.

"You're going to help me," he said quietly. "Because if anything happens to my sister, then I won't have any reason to let you live anymore, will I? I'll have nothing left to lose. Not even the state penitentiary will deter me from exacting my revenge on anybody and everybody who could have stopped bad things from happening to my sister. Besides, I hope you realize that when the Suits finally sort all this out, it's going to lead right back to you guys anyway. Are you really that sure this Jimmy kid won't squeal?"

I glanced over at Vince. Staples made a compelling

argument. That much was for sure. Plus, deep down I knew it really was the right thing to do. But not just for his sister—for all the kids involved. I had been lying to myself all this time. There was no retiring from this. Me trying to argue any further would be like a Great White shark trying to become a vegetarian. Fixing problems is what I do. It's in my bones, my DNA.

Besides, if I didn't help, then Staples was going to turn me inside out like a reversible sweatshirt. That by itself kind of made it an easy decision.

"Okay," I said. "Let's do this."

"I was wondering when you'd finally give in," Vince said. "I think you know we should have never allowed this to happen in the first place. We should have just told Jimmy no."

"Great!" Staples said, suddenly smiling. Then he punched my arm to show we were all good or something. "So where do we start?"

I rubbed my shoulder wondering why some kids learned to communicate with punching instead of words like the rest of us.

"Well, the next step is to arrange another meeting with Jimmy Two-Tone to see exactly what is going on here and why Thief Valley is even involved. But we need to get to Jimmy someplace other than in the East

Wing bathroom. Someplace he'll be more exposed and vulnerable and won't have Mitch and Justin there for protection. And especially someplace where I know the Suits won't be watching."

## Chapter 15

## Spaghetti, Meatballs, and a Giant Sword

The next day, which was a Monday, I did my best to act normal and keep my distance from Jimmy's office. The last thing I needed was to attract even more attention from the Suits. This was going to be hard enough as it was to resolve without drawing attention. But I'd deal with that problem later. First things first, and the first thing was to get to Jimmy.

After school Vince and I went home just like on any other day. Principal Dickerson followed me home in his gray sedan just like on any other day. Once home all I had to do was wait.

The phone call came at 6:12 p.m. CST.

"Yeah?" I answered.

"He's with his parents at this Italian restaurant called Michael's," Staples said. "I'll be there to get you in five. Be ready." He hung up.

We'd given Staples the job of keeping track of where Jimmy went after school. Then as soon as he was someplace in public, either with his parents or alone, we'd make our move. We needed Staples for this job since he was the only one of us with a car.

I told my parents I was going to Vince's and then went outside to meet up with Staples.

The drive to the restaurant took forever. I needed to catch Jimmy there before they left. It was too risky trying to confront him at his house because he could easily just not let me inside. But at a restaurant I could get right next to him and he'd have nowhere to run or hide.

Staples pulled up in front of Michael's Italian Ristorante after about a fifteen-minute drive. I was just hoping it wasn't too late.

"I'll be waiting down the street. Don't mess this up," Staples said with a menacing look.

I entered the restaurant at 6:34 p.m. CST.

Two men stood in the corner wearing tuxedos and playing string instruments slowly and softly like we were in some old-school Italian village. It didn't seem like a super nice or expensive restaurant in spite of the tuxedoed musicians, but it was apparently pretty popular, given how many tables were filled. The place had a relaxing charm about it that I liked.

It didn't take long to find Jimmy and his parents, since the place wasn't very big. They were seated in a red booth along the far wall—his parents seated on one side, Jimmy on the other. In the dim light they looked just like any other family out to enjoy a nice dinner. No one would suspect that at that table sat one of the most conniving kids ever born and the person apparently solely responsible for starting some sort of war between two schools that had escalated to the point where swimming pools were filled with blood, guts, and body parts (fake, but still).

"Can I help you?" the host asked. She was a cute teenager with short brown hair.

"I'm meeting someone," I said, pointing toward the back booth.

"Oh, okay, then," she said with a smile, and then stepped aside.

I made my way back toward their table. They still had food on their plates; I'd made it with time to spare. A few steps away I took a deep breath.

"Hey, Jimmy!" I said as I walked up to them.

Jimmy's eyes grew larger than the giant meatballs sitting on his plate. He dropped his fork. I could see the wheels turning inside his head.

"Oh, Jimmy," cooed his blue-eyed mom, "is this a little friend of yours from school?"

Jimmy shook his head and was about to say something, but I beat him to the punch.

"Yeah! We're partners in crime, aren't we, Jimmy?" I said. "I came to discuss our next crime . . . uh, I mean, discuss some business."

"Partners in crime?" his brown-eyed dad said, not sure if I was joking.

"He's only kidding, Dad," Jimmy said quickly. "Could we, like, sit alone for a second?"

His mom looked uncertain.

"You know, Mom, middle-school stuff!" Jimmy said.

I saw his dad motion toward his mom that they should move.

"Oh, okay, Mom and Dad will go sit at the bar for a little bit," she said.

"Dad is glad you're making friends, Jimmy," his dad said.

I marveled at the fact that his parents also did that weird refer-to-themselves-by-their-own-names thing—something Vince told me was called speaking in the third person. Which made no sense since it only involved one person, but whatever. The point is this: his whole family was nuts.

Jimmy's mom and dad got up and took their plates of

food and drinks to the small bar at the front of the restaurant. Then it was just Jimmy, me, a half-eaten plate of spaghetti and meatballs, and a candle.

I sat down across from Jimmy Two-Tone and folded my hands in front of me. I started by just staring at him without blinking. Something I'd learned from watching lots of mobster movies and TV shows about training dogs: unflinching eye contact shows your dominance. I tried my best not to blink or smile or even move as I stared Jimmy down in the booth across from me.

He shifted in his seat several times as he tried to match my stare, but he was clearly uncomfortable. Nervous, even. Then he broke eye contact first, losing the battle of dominance. He stuck his fork in his spaghetti and seemed to collect himself a little bit. He took a huge bite that left red lines of sauce all over his cheeks.

"What do you want, guy? Jimmy's trying to enjoy a nice dinner with his family," he said with his mouth still full, spraying bits of meatball and noodles and sauce all over the white paper covering the table.

He was much less professional at the dinner table than when doing business.

I noticed that there were crayons lying near his plate. I'd seen this before at other restaurants. Sometimes they had huge sheets of white paper instead of normal tablecloths and then they gave your table crayons so you could draw on it. I noticed a few drawings that Jimmy had apparently done as well as a few games of hangman they'd apparently played as a family.

Jimmy's drawings were of a dog chewing on a ball and an eyeball floating in space with a small stickman looking up at it. And one drawing was of a cat sitting in a window. They were surprisingly good drawings.

Jimmy noticed me looking at them, and he shifted his plate so that most of the drawings were covered.

"Jimmy," I said finally, having let enough silence sit between us to show off my power over him, "when you get into a business like this and you're not totally honest with people, bad things tend to happen."

Jimmy looked at me and then swallowed before shoving more noodles into his mouth and chewing again.

"What do you mean by that, bro?" he asked, spraying more bits of food onto the table again. "Jimmy doesn't like riddles. Jimmy prefers, like, straight-up talking, dude."

I reached over and grabbed his plate and slid it across the table and just out of his reach. He looked at me like he wanted to jab his fork into my hand. I picked up a gray crayon and a black crayon.

"This is what I mean," I said.

I drew a black cat like the one in his drawing—mine wasn't nearly as good, but it looked enough like his that

I'm sure he would get the point. Then with the gray crayon I drew a huge knife sticking out of the cat's back. If there'd have been a red crayon, I'd have drawn some blood for effect.

"Hey, bud, are you threatening Jimmy's cat? 'Cause that ain't cool, man, if you are," Jimmy said, looking nervous. "Jimmy and his cat don't like threats, guy."

"No, not me, Jimmy. The people you're making back-alley deals with to mess up our school! I don't have anything against you or your cat, aside from you giving this business a dirty name, but that's beside the point. What I'm trying to say is when you make back-alley deals and double-cross people, bad things will happen."

With that I circled the picture I'd drawn.

"Look, friend, Jimmy doesn't know what you're talking about! Why would you stab Jimmy's cat, Scarface, with that, like, jumbo sword?"

Of course his cat's name was Scarface. That was too obvious. Only a *Scarface* fan would think to do something like that. I bet that like 90 percent of *Scarface* fans had at least one pet named Tony or Scarface.

"This is what I'm talking about," I said.

I took out my phone and set it on the table. I pressed Play on the video clip Tyrell had forwarded me. He'd edited it so first you see the Swimming Pool Bloodbath

Massacre in all its gory glory, then it cuts to two kids sneaking around near some bushes behind the school with bags of supplies that could be used to create a fake cannibal holocaust, then it cuts to them clearly being handed cash-size envelopes from Jimmy under a street-light with the school clearly visible in the background. All were time-stamped with the same date and within a few hours of each other.

"So, want to tell me why you're making back-alley deals with kids from Thief Valley? Because I really need to know. I hand you my business and then you apparently pay to purposefully sabotage it and yourself? It doesn't make any sense, Jimmy."

Jimmy buried his face in his hands and shook his head.

"Look," he said, "Jimmy wasn't trying to sabotage his own business, guy. He was trying to *help* it."

"I don't get it," I said.

"Look, friend, right after you handed the business over to me, I was approached by this huge dude who claimed to be representing a rival business owner over at Thief Valley Elementary. Some guy named Ken-Co apparently has an operation pretty similar up there at TV. Ever heard of him?"

I shook my head. This was news to me. I was actually shocked. I had no idea that there was another business just like mine less than fifteen miles away.

"Well," Jimmy continued, "he's apparently a pretty big deal over there. Makes this business look like a game of hopscotch. So they make Jimmy this offer he can't refuse, right, dude? I mean, they say they'll cause some problems and drum up some business for me in exchange for a small cut of the profits. And Jimmy is thinking, Well, what better way to make a splash with this new business than to show kids right away what Jimmy is capable of, right?"

I just looked at him and waited.

"Anyway, as you know, guy, this is a volume-based business. It's all about the numbers you can churn through. So Jimmy figures this deal is perfect. It's more money all around—more for you and Vince, more for this Ken-Co guy, and more for Jimmy. Win-win-win. But that's when things start to go wrong. At first it works like a charm, but then this Ken-Co guy starts doing too much. The problems he's creating are more than Jimmy can handle. Pretty soon Jimmy owes this guy money. Mac, I just . . . I can't pay my debts. Jimmy's in deep now. It just got so out of hand. I don't know why he double-crossed me like this. I really don't."

I shook my head. "How deep are you in?"

"Close to four grand," Jimmy said.

My head about smashed into the table. *Four thousand*

*dollars?* That was insane! How could he have gotten that behind?

"You really think that if I don't pay him back soon, he'll, like, stab Scarface with some giant momma-jamma sword?" he said, glancing nervously at my drawing.

"Yeah, exactly like that," I said.

"Dude," he said.

I nodded.

"Guy," he said, shaking his head in disbelief.

"Why didn't you come to me sooner?" I said.

"Because I knew you wanted to be retired. And, well, Jimmy was kind of embarrassed. Your reputation is a lot to live up to, bro."

I shook my head and sighed.

"Tell me more about this Ken-Co," I said.

"Well, Jimmy never really met the guy before. I only met his assistant, but Jimmy heard he's a pretty ruthless guy. I guess he runs a pretty good business. But I don't think he's going to stop sabotaging our school anytime soon."

Out of the corner of my eye I saw his parents get up and start heading this way.

"All right, Jimmy, I'll be in touch soon," I said, and then got up to leave.

"Are you going to help me?"

"We'll see," I said, and then walked past his parents and out the door.

Once outside the restaurant I had to restrain myself from picking up this little dog that some guy was walking and punting it right through the restaurant window. Okay, okay, I'd never actually hurt a dog—I loved dogs—but being that angry can put crazy thoughts into people's heads. I mean, he owed over four thousand dollars? How was that even possible to owe someone that much in just a few weeks? And how was I ever going to find a way to fix this?

# Chapter 16

# Hole in One

The next evening Vince, Staples, and I went to play miniature golf. It was another one of Staples's "brownie point" outings. I wasn't sure where the phrase "brownie points" came from, but I was starting to pretty much hate it. Because in our case it didn't involve scoring any points or eating any brownies. For us it simply meant getting slugged in the limbs a lot. Well, okay, maybe Staples had stopped doing that as much now that he knew his sister was mixed up in some sort of school war.

And so, yeah, maybe he wasn't quite the same blood-thirsty psycho he had been a year ago, but he was still plenty mean when he wanted to be. And being around him made me nervous. I mean, could anyone blame me if I never would truly trust the guy again?

"So I think the next step is that I should meet up with this Ken-Co kid to see if we can make a bargain with him somehow. I mean, paying him back in full will be basically impossible." I hit my ball toward this ramp that would send it soaring over a mini waterfall. It was a pretty cool mini-golf course that Staples had taken us to; I'd give him that much.

"Wait, you have enough to cover it, don't you?" Staples said as he watched my ball sail not only over the waterfall but also right over the hole and bounce off some rocks that were technically out of bounds. "I mean, what happened to all your cash? You guys used to be loaded."

I glanced at Vince, who was pretending to study the hole we were on.

Our dwindling cash supply was a touchy subject with him. Not because he was greedy or obsessed with money, necessarily. He was just overly cautious. It stressed him out anytime our cash dropped under three thousand dollars because a good business always has a lot of disposable cash or something like that. I usually zoned out when Vince would get into one of his financial mumbo-jumbo lectures.

"We've spent most of it," I said. "Some cleaning up the mess last year, some just for fun over the summer, and some paying out old debts to longtime employees like Joe and Tyrell. Stuff like that. Plus, the Cubs are terrible again, so the Game Fund just didn't feel worth keeping anymore. And yeah, we've been getting a cut from Jimmy, but a cut is still just a cut. Fifteen percent does not equal four grand, not even in the best of years, and this has only been, what, like a month, maybe? How much money *do* we have left, anyway, Vince?"

I had a general idea, but Vince was our money guy so he'd know for sure.

"Last I checked we were down to $1612.86 in all of our Funds combined," Vince said. "Those are all of our liquid assets."

"That's it?" Staples said as he drained his second putt into the cup.

"Hey, it goes faster than you realize when there's not as much money coming in," I said, scooping my ball out of the hole after logging a six.

Staples just shook his head in disbelief. I could see why he was shocked. Way back when he'd stolen all of our Funds, there'd been over six grand all combined. We were worth just a fraction of what we used to be.

"Where does that leave us?" Staples asked.

"I think I'll have to go pay this Ken-Co a visit. To see if we can work out some sort of deal or payment plan or something. I mean, he runs a pretty good business from the sound of it, so I'm sure he's a reasonable dude. Besides, he's only a fourth or fifth grader, supposedly."

"I still can't believe we're digging Jimmy out of this pro bono," Vince said.

"Well, it's more about helping Staples and all the other kids than it is helping Jimmy, but I know what you mean. It does feel like he's getting a free ride here, doesn't it? We'll probably have to neutralize him somehow once this is all over."

"And I also can't believe we're getting involved again. I mean, we could have been out, Mac!"

"I know, but what choice do we have now? The only thing left that we can do is fix this and then get the business shut down for good. Ken-Co can have this town if he wants; our school has to be out after this, completely."

As I said that, I hit my ball and it passed through a mechanical alligator's opening and closing mouth, came out the tail, and dropped into the cup.

"Yeah!" I said. "Hole in one!"

I jumped up and did a celebratory dance like I'd just scored a touchdown. I was really just kidding around; I didn't care that much about a game of mini golf.

"Nice job, buddy," Staples said, and then proceeded to slug me in the arm so hard that my celebration instantly came to a close and I almost went tumbling down the side of the fake miniature mountain that the course was built on.

Vince laughed at me and lined up for his putt.

As Staples walked by him, he clipped Vince's putter with his own during Vince's backswing, and Vince's ball ricocheted off the side wall and bounced down the side of the mountain we'd been working our way up.

Now it was Staples's turn to laugh as Vince sighed and started off down the mountain to retrieve his ball, apologizing to other golfers as he stepped across neighboring holes. I shook my head. We needed to get this mess resolved before Staples accidentally killed us while goofing around. I could just see the headline now: LOCAL TEEN'S ARM EXPLODES FOLLOWING RECEIPT OF 158TH CONSECUTIVE PUNCH.

# Chapter 17

## My-Me

That Wednesday I took a sick day from school in order to go pay Ken-Co a visit at Thief Valley Elementary. If his business was anything like mine, then the only way I could get an appointment was to show up on a school day. Which was risky business for me.

First, it meant I had to sneak around another school even though I wasn't a student there. In my experience, schools typically don't like random people, especially those older than their students (like me), just hanging around and acting suspiciously. It gives off the wrong kind of vibe, and if I was caught, it would almost definitely get back to Dickerson somehow. I was pretty sure that all principals were not only friends outside of work, but probably had some sort of Secret Suit Society that met every other Saturday night in a clearing in the woods behind the local Walmart. They all probably wore bathrobes over their business suits and sieves as hats, and recited enchantments and cast spells on their especially challenging troublemakers, and boiled cauldrons full of burned coffee and giggled and ate popcorn, and told stories, and then finished with a rousing game of truth or dare before sacrificing a goat to Principal Emperor Mr. Belding. You never could know for sure with principals.

And the other reason that it was risky was that I had to skip school. Because school was obviously not like your parents' jobs where they just get vacation days. I mean, all absences needed to be excused somehow. Especially for me with Dickerson all over me like he had been. Luckily getting kids out of school used to be one of my specialties. It was one of the more popular requests I got back when I'd run my business.

When kids needed a way out of school, I always called in Mike "My-Me" Winslow. He was the master of impressions. He could impersonate anyone or anything. In class he once did this impression of a squeaky wheel every time the teacher sat in her chair.

It sounded so real that the teacher kept calling down to the office to get the chair fixed. The teacher called down so many times that eventually the school just bought her a whole new chair. Then when she sat in the new chair for the first time My-Me did the squeaking noise again, but this time just slightly different. The look on the teacher's face was one of the funniest things I'd ever seen in my life. Even though I did feel kind of bad for her—I mean, I definitely hoped My-Me's prank didn't have anything to do with this teacher's mental breakdown later that year where she showed up to school wearing waffles on her feet and shoes on her hands.

So, anyways, the thing was My-Me could impersonate adult voices so well that the attendance secretary never called the parents at work to verify that the sick calls were real like she sometimes did if the call sounded suspicious in any way. Part of his trick, in addition to just the awesome adult sound of his impressions, was that he was the master of using weird phrases and words that only old people used, such as: "I'm afraid he's come down with a case of the chills" or "He's sick as a dog" or "She's a bit under the weather today."

So my day started with an early morning phone call to My-Me. He was used to this. My waking him at six or sometimes even five in the morning for emergency cases was something he was typically well-compensated for in our past dealings.

"Mac. Haven't heard from you in a while," he said, sounding half-asleep still.

"Yeah, well, as you know, I'm not really in business anymore."

"Yeah, exactly, so what's up?" He didn't sound angry or annoyed but definitely curious as to why I'd interrupted his dreams a full hour before he probably normally woke up each morning.

"I need a personal favor this time, one which you'll still be paid the usual fee for," I said.

"You need a sick call for yourself?" he asked, sounding surprised.

I'd never actually had My-Me call me personally in sick before. I'd always made it a habit to not miss school in the past, since, when you had a business operation like the one I'd been running for the past five years, missing school meant lost business. Lost business meant lost profits.

"You up for it?"

"Hey!" he said, transforming his voice into that of a shouting forty-year-old dude from Brooklyn, an impression of this old comedian that he sometimes did. "Hey!

What do I look like? A sausage? Of course I'm up for it! Hey!"

I laughed. "Great. Just give me the standard sick call. One day is all I need."

"Hey, you got it, pal," he said, still in character. "Hey!"

# Chapter 18

## School Yard Scrum

**S**taples dropped me off a few blocks away from Thief Valley around nine o'clock. I'd walk the rest of the way. Staples wanted to keep his distance from his sister's school during the week until he got the go-ahead from the courts to have official custody. Apparently, he'd been involved in some pretty unsavory business here in the past.

"See you," I said as I got out of his car.

I didn't really have much of a plan yet. I had plenty of experience at breaking into schools, but always my own. And I usually had a key. I had zero experience doing anything at other schools except for going to sports events and playing baseball games. I didn't even know where Ken-Co's office was or how to find him.

But I was sure I'd think of something. I always did.

From the outside it looked like any other school. The outside looked pretty quiet. I was guessing morning recess would be around ten o'clock. I would probably keep my distance until then and scope the place out.

After circling the school, I'd discovered that it had five entrances/exits, one playground, one junky base-ball field (if you could call it that), and two small parking lots. Recess was likely going to be my best shot to get in undetected, since I could probably just blend in with the other kids.

It seemed to take forever for recess to arrive. I was waiting across the street behind a row of bushes in somebody's front yard. I kept sneaking glances at the house behind me, worried that the owner might come running out and chase me off with a rake or something. Or sic a bloodthirsty rottweiler on me. Or even worse, call the cops.

But there wasn't any activity from inside that I could see. Well, at least not at first. Probably the third time I looked back, there was a kid in the window. He was young, probably too young to be in school yet, but old enough to stand and walk and maybe talk. His face and shoulders were all I could see, and he was like a statue, just staring at me with a blank expression on his face. I almost ran but was too creeped out to even move at all. The worst part was that the kid was wearing a black suit and tie. What kind of five-year-old wears a suit at nine thirty in the morning?

I tried to ignore his stare. When I turned to face the school, I could still feel it boring into me like a laser. I glanced back again. He was still there, not moving, not smiling. Nothing. Just staring.

Thief Valley gave me the creeps.

Just when I thought I couldn't take it anymore, I heard the recess bell from across the street. I made my move, darting out from behind the bushes. I had to time this perfectly or I'd be noticed.

I ran across the street and ducked behind a car in the parking lot nearest the playground. A few kids were starting to trickle outside now, as well as a few recess supervisors. I moved closer, staying behind the parked cars.

Then suddenly there was another kid right next to me, crouching behind the car.

I gasped and almost ate some gravel. But I gathered myself enough to say, "Tyrell?"

The kid looked at me and raised his eyebrows. "Who?"

Now that I had a better look at him, I realized it wasn't Tyrell at all. But he had looked like him for just a second. And more than that, Tyrell was the only kid I knew who could sneak up and get within inches of me without making a single noise.

"Sorry, I thought you were someone else."

"Nope, not Someone Else. My name's LT," he said, offering his hand.

I didn't know many grade-school kids that shook hands when meeting someone unless they were making business deals, but I shrugged and shook it anyway. "Zack."

I figured there was no benefit from telling him my real name.

"Okay, 'Zack,'" he said, putting a weird emphasis on my fake name, clearly not buying it, "want to tell me why you've been across the street spying on our school for the past half hour? Not to mention making a sweep around the outside as if taking inventory?"

"I . . . ," I started, but stopped.

The truth was I didn't know what to say.

"Right," he said. "Well, just let me warn you, whatever you got going on, man, you best be careful. Ken-Co doesn't really appreciate uninvited guests hanging out around the school, you know."

I nodded, relieved that it seemed like he wasn't going to turn me in for whatever reason. Then as suddenly as he'd arrived, he was gone. So I guessed Ken-Co had his own version of Tyrell. That partially explained why he ran such a good operation. A business is only as good as its employees.

The sound of a full-fledged recess in progress turned my attention back to the mission at hand. I realized I probably should have asked LT where to find Ken-Co, but I'd been too stunned to even think of it. I peeked at the playground; hundreds of kids played on equipment, lounged around talking, or were playing a variety of other games near the baseball field.

I came out from behind the car and ran to the edge of the building. As soon as I was sure both recess supervisors were not looking, I casually walked out from behind the school and sauntered my way into the crowds of kids.

There were kids of all different ages and heights and sizes. I tried to group myself near the biggest of them, who were mostly just standing around talking and joking in between the slide and the baseball field's outfield. Luckily for me, I was still pretty short for a seventh grader, so I didn't stick out among the fifth and sixth graders. Well, at least not at first glance. It was pretty clear right away that the kids noticed I didn't belong here.

"Hey, kid, who are you?" asked one of them. A particularly big and hairy grade schooler who looked kind of like Sasquatch. In fact, the word "Yeti" was literally written all over his face in huge and elaborate black lettering. I couldn't tell if it was a tattoo or if he just had a really bad self-drawing habit.

Either way, I ignored him and joined a group of four kids and pretended to laugh at one of their jokes. They made faces at me that said stuff like "Who is this geek?" The whole thing was about as awkward as it sounds, but I didn't know what else to do. I clearly was not as good at this kind of stuff as Tyrell. I didn't know what I'd been expecting, but this was definitely going a lot worse than I'd imagined. This type of stuff always looked way easier in the movies.

A hand grabbed my shoulder and spun me around.

"Hey, kid, I was talking to you," Sasquatch said. "What are you doing here, huh?"

Even though he was younger than me (well, unless he'd been held back a few years, that is, which is entirely possible considering his flat caveman head and soft feathery mustache), he was still at least several inches taller.

"Me?" I said, trying to sound offended.

"Yeah, you!"

There was a group forming around us now. This wasn't going well. Not at all.

"Hey, I'm new here. It's my first day," I said, trying to look like a terrified fifth grader.

"He's lying!" someone in the crowd shouted.

Were TV kids clairvoyant? I mean, they'd sniffed me out like I was wearing a vest made of fish heads under my clothes or something. It would have been almost laughable were I not getting pretty concerned that Sasquatch was going to take out his anger about using such poor judgment in getting "Yeti" labeled all over his face on my relatively small head.

Then Sasquatch shoved me. I kept my balance only because I crashed into the wall of kids behind me who just shoved me back into the middle of the circle of kids that had formed. Sasquatch laughed and so did a lot of the crowd.

"Okay, okay," I said. "Look, I just came here to see Ken—"

But I couldn't finish my sentence because it's hard to talk when a giant hairy fist is smashing into your mouth. Sasquatch's totally unprovoked punch knocked me back and definitely stunned me, but I was still on my feet. I tasted some blood where my lip had split open slightly.

"Fight!" someone yelled.

The crowd grew as Sasquatch came at me again. This time I was able to duck easily under his wild right hook. As I passed him, I clipped the side of his heel with my foot. He sprawled onto the dirt. Kids booed, some yelled, and some cheered, likely just for the fight itself rather than for me specifically.

How the heck did I get myself into a fight within thirty seconds of being here? The kids of Thief Valley were just a bunch of hairy, creepy, suit-wearing, face-tattooing, bloodthirsty psychos. Sasquatch climbed to his feet with a scowl on his face that distorted one of the "Yeti"s on his face into a "Yet." He let out a short scream of pure primordial rage like he really was a giant mountain-dwelling beast.

I figured I was about to find myself flying about eighty feet through the air, but an authoritative voice silenced all of us.

"What is going on here?" one of the recess supervisors shouted.

The crowd parted, and she came lumbering in between me and Sasquatch. She saw the scrapes on his elbows and then grabbed my arm firmly, before I even had a chance to make a break for it.

"He tripped me," Sasquatch said, and then started crying.

I was impressed by his instant waterworks but also disgusted that he'd stoop that low. He was a BNT (bull-n-tell), the absolute worst kind of bully of them all. The sort of kid who just bullied other kids mercilessly and then as soon as anyone ever tried to fight back, they'd start crying and tattle.

"He punched me first," I said, pointing at my lip with my free hand.

The recess supervisor looked at me. I thought she was studying my lip, but it turns out she was looking for something else.

"You don't go to school here," she said, ignoring my split lip altogether.

"Yes, I do," I said, knowing the lie was weak, but it was my only hope.

"No, he doesn't," a few kids from the crowd said. "He doesn't go here."

What was with the kids here? Narcs, all of them.

"Whose class are you in?" she asked, her beady eyes glowing a smug *I Told You So*.

"Uh, Mrs. Johnson's?" I tried.

"Oh really?" she asked.

I nodded.

"So I'm supposed to believe that you're in first grade, then?"

I nodded again, not knowing what else to do. All of my guts had melted now, along with my lungs and brain. They were all pooled inside my legs, making them weak. It took everything I had not to just collapse. There was no way out of this now.

"Yeah," I said in a voice that was clearly trying way too

hard to sound like a first grader. "I want my mommy!"

A few kids laughed at my pathetic attempt to sound like a first grader, but the recess supervisor was not amused. I could tell by the way she was baring her teeth at me like a snarling dog.

"Well, what you're going to get is a trip to the principal's office and then probably a trip to your own school's principal," she said.

And just like that it was all over. I was going to be expelled.

## Chapter 19

# Dead Man Walking

The recess supervisor never let go of my arm as she led me through the side doors. In fact, her grip seemed to get tighter as we went deeper into the school. The inside was kind of like my school in some ways, but then in many other ways not like it at all.

It stunk, for one. Literally. I didn't know what my school smelled like, probably not good either, but this one smelled really funny. And not funny ha-ha. It smelled like a mixture of beef gravy and Urinal Cocktail (you know, it's that thing that sometimes happens in boys' bathrooms where no one flushes a particular urinal for a while and then everyone keeps using that same one like we're all involved in some sort of unwritten contract together to see if we can make it overflow).

I felt numb as we went down halls, around corners, and past classrooms, likely on our way to the administration offices. I could barely keep up with my captor as she charged ahead. Luckily she pulled me along hard every time I started lagging. I couldn't believe I was going to be expelled over this. Just like that. I mean, I was *retired*. This was exactly why I had quit, too. This sort of thing wasn't supposed to happen to kids who had retired.

A few kids were in the halls. They stopped and stared as we passed. Teachers we came across looked at me sullenly and shook their heads slowly. Was it just me or did this school's lights seem to be a lot dimmer than at my school? It seemed like the lighting was only getting darker as we moved deeper into the school, too.

I was looking up at the lights, trying to figure out why it seemed so dark, when suddenly water splashed on my face and the recess supervisor let go of my arm. Her right shoulder and face were drenched, and a broken and deflated rubber balloon stuck to the curls of her dark hair. Then, seemingly out of nowhere, another balloon soared in and nailed her in the right leg. She jumped back, rage engulfing her face. We were being assaulted.

"Run!" I heard a voice yell.

I didn't need another prompt. I took off sprinting

down the hall in the direction we'd just come from.

"Hey!" I heard the recess supervisor shout at me.

I glanced back just as another water balloon pelted her in the back of the head. She turned around to see who her assailants were, but the hall looked empty. They were good, whoever they were. I darted left down another hallway. The recess supervisor, frozen with indecision between going after me or her assailants, had a ton of ground to make up now if she ended up choosing to chase me.

I wasn't going to waste my lead. I weaved in and out of the halls, looking for an exit or place to hide. A teacher popped out of a classroom as I passed. He started walking after me.

"Hey," he said. "Hey!"

I bolted left around another corner. This place was like a maze. I just needed to find an empty hallway where I wouldn't be seen entering a room of some kind. From there, well, I'd figure out what to do, but I just needed to find a good hiding spot to collect my thoughts.

If everything else so far that morning had gone about as bad as could be expected, then you couldn't blame me for being shocked at my fortune when I rounded the next corner to find a completely deserted intersection in the hallway. I knew the one teacher was probably still walking after me and maybe the recess supervisor, too, so I had to act fast.

The left branch was a long hallway that stretched for what seemed like infinity with a billion doors. The right branch was much shorter with about five doors, including a glowing green exit sign posted above the last one on the left. I needed to decide now whether to cut my losses and make a break for it or stick around and try to carry out the mission. I heard footsteps approaching behind me.

I moved quickly down the shorter hallway to my right, glancing at the doors as I passed them. The first few were definitely classrooms. I wasn't about to try to hide in a regular classroom. I was likely only seconds away from giving up and bolting for the exit when I caught my second break.

The second-to-last door on the right looked to be an old storage room of some kind. It still had a long, narrow glass window like the other classrooms, but instead of regular rows of desks and chairs the dark room just held a bunch of boxes, piles of chairs, and really old wooden desks.

I tried the handle and was somewhat shocked to find it unlocked. It seemed as though my luck was turning in an epic reversal of fortune that could probably be matched only by three straight Chicago Cubs World Series titles.

I slipped inside and shut the door behind me as quietly and quickly as I could.

The room was dark, but the light coming in through the small window in the door was just enough for me to avoid tripping over any boxes or clutter as I moved toward the back. I heard the bell ring, signaling the end of recess. I found a large pile of boxes near the back and wedged myself in behind them. And . . .

Well . . .

Now what?

I wasn't really sure at all what I was supposed to do next. I still intended to try to meet with Ken-Co if I could and fulfill what I came here to do. But how? I mean, here I was hiding behind stacks of boxes. How was this going to help me?

Hopefully, anybody who had been chasing me would just assume after enough time looking that I'd exited the building and was gone. I heard the faint noises of kids moving through the halls, heading back to class. Well, I was guessing there wasn't much more I'd be able to do until lunch, since likely Ken-Co and all of his employees would have to be in class until then.

I sighed.

At least I'd found a relatively safe place to hide until then. I could use this free time to try and figure out exactly what my next move should be. I took out my phone and played a game to kill some time and help clear my thoughts. Sometimes my best brainstorming was done while mindlessly fidgeting with my phone or playing a game. Besides, I likely couldn't make another move until lunch so I had tons of time to kill. Two hours may not actually be all that long, but when you're cramped in the corner of a dark storage room alone, two hours is basically a lifetime.

I was just starting to settle in when the door to the storage room opened. I pocketed my phone as quickly as I could, careful not to make any noise. I only hoped whoever it was hadn't seen the glow of the screen first.

"Well, he definitely came down this way," a man's voice said.

The lights flicked on, and I had to shut my eyes tightly and cover my face from the sudden blinding glare. I had been getting used to the dark.

"Who is he?" another male voice asked.

"I don't know, but he was outside bullying our students," said a voice that I recognized as that of the recess supervisor.

So they clearly hadn't given up their search, after all. And look what I'd done. I'd had my chance to escape, but instead I'd chosen to corner myself in this room like a penned animal at one of those horrible hunting farms where basically rich, dumb people who want to pretend they're hunters pay to go inside a large fenced area and shoot defenseless animals.

And here I was, stupider than those animals who probably didn't even end up in those pens by choice like I had. Idiot. I smacked my forehead with my open palm without realizing what I was doing.

"What was that?" one of the men said.

"Probably a cockroach, knowing this place," the other guy said, and then all three of them laughed.

I heard them start to shuffle through the boxes and clutter at the front of the room. I probably only had a matter of minutes before I'd be discovered. I went through my options.

I could make a break for it. If I moved quickly, I might catch them off guard and be able to slip right by them and out into the hallway.

I could grab a plastic chair and fight them to the death.

I could try to use the Force and conjure up some sort of crazy tornado of boxes, desks, and junk and use it to tear a hole in the roof that I would then fly out of.

I could just keep sitting here thinking about ridiculous scenarios until I was caught, turned in to Dickerson, and expelled.

As much as I hated to admit it, option four seemed to be the most likely to occur. One of the searchers was just around the pile of junk now. It was the recess supervisor; I could hear her heavy breathing, like a siren warning an impending storm.

Then I felt a hand grab the back of my shirt. The wall I'd been sitting against was suddenly gone, and I was falling backward into the dark.

# Chapter 20

## The Australian Darkness

It all happened so fast, it took me a while to figure out that I hadn't actually just plummeted into some spontaneous black hole and would never be heard from again. The first thing that clued me in was the voice of a kid speaking right next to me.

"That were a close one, eh, mate?" he whispered with a thick Australian accent.

It was pitch-black. I mean the kind of dark where the only thing I could actually see was the inside of my eyelids when I closed them. It was also sort of cramped; I could feel that much. There was enough room for me to sit upright, as I currently was, but I could feel my hair brushing against a hard surface above us.

"Where are we?" I whispered. "What happened?"

He snickered quietly. "Come on. It'll all come good," he said.

With his accent and everything I didn't really know what exactly he meant. But I heard him shuffling down the cramped tunnel to my right. Or at least I hoped that was him and not some sort of giant Thief Valley School rat.

"You coming or what, mate?" he whispered again, except this time his voice was several feet farther away.

"I can't see," I said back.

He laughed again. "Aw, well, lucky for you there's only two ways to go."

Then he started moving again. He had a point. And I definitely didn't want to get stuck in here alone and end up some cryptic skeleton that would be found someday in the year, like, 2079 and make everybody wonder just how this strange small boy got stuck inside the walls of a school.

I quickly crawled after the Australian kid, wondering how and why I'd been saved twice by the students here. Especially after it had been their fault I'd been caught in the first place. The ground under my palms was cold and hard, with very little dirt or dust considering we were inside of a wall. Why would a crawl space behind a wall be paved?

"Are we going to see Ken-Co?" I asked.

"Maybe," he said. I could tell he was having fun with me.

"So he runs a pretty good business, then, huh?"

At this the Aussie simply laughed. He laughed so loud it echoed through the tunnel and sounded like ten kids were laughing instead of just one.

When he was finished laughing, he stopped ahead of me.

"Mate?" he said.

"Yeah?"

"It's the best business this side of Brisbane, Australia. It runs like a machine. Every piece oiled, every employee loyal. Nothing ever breaks down, ever. You see, money does all our talking for us, and we answer to no one. We own this school, the teachers, the janitor; I even heard we got the superintendent under our thumb."

If this was true, then I was dealing with a businessman the likes of which I'd never come close to knowing. Even Staples's empire in its greatest moments was like a dude selling fake designer purses on the sidewalk compared to what this kid was describing.

"All right. Let's go, then, yes?" he said, and kept moving.

After what must have been a hundred yards of

crawling through narrow spaces and around corners, he stopped.

Then a small flashlight clicked on, which blinded me for a few seconds. After my eyes adjusted, I saw that we were at a fork. One branch of the small cement tunnel went left and seemed to gradually get bigger farther down the path. The right branch stayed pretty small and actually seemed to slope down, as if it led to an underground level.

"Kinda creepy-looking, isn't it, mate?" he said, tilting his head toward the right branch.

"That's where we're headed, isn't it?" I said.

He responded only by laughing again, and then he started down the narrow tunnel. I sighed and then followed.

The slope was pretty gradual at first, but after a little bit it got a lot steeper, and I felt my hands slipping on the cement. It was getting tough to keep from slamming face-first into the Australian kid's heels. Then, just when I was sure I was at my breaking point, that I was about to get my teeth knocked out by his shoes or the cement floor, he was suddenly gone.

We finally exited the tunnel as it'd turned in to a larger room. I heard about all the bones in my body cracking and popping like fireworks as I climbed to my feet.

The room was cement and probably the size of a normal school classroom. There were no windows of any kind, and I assumed that we were likely at least partway underground now. Light came from six or seven flashlights and battery-powered camping lanterns hanging on the walls throughout the room.

Beside the passage we'd just come from, I could see at least two other small openings, as well as an open door leading into another chamber. The Australian kid stood next to me, watching my face and wearing that stupid grin of his. Two pretty big kids stood on either side of the open door. They were also studying me.

One of them was a girl and one a guy, but other than that they looked almost identical. They were clearly twins.

"We've been expecting you," the girl said.

"What took so long?" her brother said.

The Australian kid shrugged. "I couldn't find the bugger! He ran off and then hid in the three twenty-two storage room. It took me a few minutes to figure out where he'd gone."

The twins seemed to accept this as an okay excuse because the girl handed him something that I was guessing was money. Then the Australian kid turned to me and said, "Well, good luck, mate. You'll need it."

Before I could ask what he meant by that, he was gone, scurrying off through one of the small tunnel openings in the wall.

I looked at the twins. The guy smiled at me in a smug way, as if he wanted me to know that he knew what was in store for me and that he also knew that I didn't know what he knew. This kid was good at giving looks that said a lot.

The girl didn't smile. She just stared at me.

"You've been expecting me?" I asked. "How is that possible?"

They didn't answer. Instead the guy motioned toward the door between them.

"This way," he said.

What was it with TV kids and being so reluctant to answer questions directly?

I followed the kids into the next chamber, which was roughly the same size and had a similar setup, including several small tunnel openings and two more metal doors. There was also a small printed sign a few feet from one of the doors that said, "The Line Starts Here ➜ "

One of those red-velvet, movie-theater ropes used to partition lines at giant cinemas ran along the wall behind the sign. Nobody was in line at the moment, which made sense since it was regular class time. Speaking of, just how was it possible that all these kids were out of class without getting in trouble? There was a reason my business operated only during recess and lunch: it just wouldn't be possible to get out of class regularly during other times of the day. I was annoyed that Ken-Co had achieved this, and I was probably a little jealous, too.

The guy pounded on the metal door opposite the sign. In the enclosed cement chamber the clanging almost sounded like thunder. His twin sister folded her sizable arms and continued to stare at me like she thought I might have insulted her but wasn't quite sure.

"Pretty nice setup you guys have," I said, trying to sound as nice as possible.

"Hmm" was her reply.

I heard a muffled voice from inside the metal door but couldn't make out what it said. Then the guy turned to me and opened the door. He smiled and motioned for me to head inside the room.

"She's been expecting you," he said.

# Chapter 21

## Ken-Co

*She?* Was this not Ken-Co that I was going to see?

"Come on, she doesn't have all day," the twin sister said, her arms still folded.

I swallowed, but there was no point since I didn't think my mouth had produced a single drop of saliva since my split lip had crusted over about a half hour ago. Then I walked past the twins and into the next room.

It was smaller than the other chambers but still fairly large. It was about the size of a normal business-man's office, based on what I'd seen in movies. Besides the door I'd just walked through, there was one other metal door in the center of the wall to my right. A single electric, fluorescent lantern hung from the ceiling. The walls themselves were covered in posters of bands and movies and musicians, most of them bands and movies containing teen pop stars and actors from Nickelodeon shows. There were also a few shelves on the wall to my left housing several dozen unicorn toys and figurines.

In the middle of the small room sat a large wooden desk. Well, it actually wasn't all that large; it just looked large because the girl sitting behind it was so small. Her head was down, but I could tell she was in, like, probably third grade, fourth at the absolute most. There was no way she was Ken-Co, the businessperson so good, his or her operation had a whole network of underground tunnels, right? And don't think it's because she was a girl either. I mean, with what Hannah Kjelson had put me through the year before I knew never to underestimate girls. Besides, as the old saying goes: "In grade school girls are more dangerous than shotguns."

No, I was shocked because she was so young. I mean, when I was her age, my business had been nowhere near this level.

"Are you going to sit down or what?" she asked.

I could see her feet dangling slightly off the ground under the desk. The desk was so tall that she had to sit in a regular adult-sized chair to fit it. It was actually a huge, old, ornate chair, almost like a throne or some-thing. Her feet kicked back and forth slowly like she was on some kind of Saturday afternoon joyride in her parents' convertible.

I sat down in the much smaller chair across from her.

It was only at this moment that I noticed someone else was in the room, too. The gargantuan excuse for a grade-school kid that I saw terrorizing kids when Vince and I came to Thief Valley with Staples stood behind Ken-Co and a little to her left, my right. He wore mirror aviator sunglasses, and if I couldn't have seen his mas-sive chest heaving slightly with each breath, he might as well have been a statue. What did they put in the water in Thief Valley anyway? HGH? Steroids? Some crazy cocktail containing both?

Her desk was stacked neatly with notebooks and binders, a single lamp that wasn't plugged in to any-thing, and a teddy bear. Which might have been cute if it hadn't been missing its eyeballs. Instead of fake eyes or button eyes this bear had only two dark holes with a few loose strands of white cotton poking out as if they were drowning inside and were begging to be pulled free.

"Oh, that?" she said, not looking up. "That was a gift from my brother a long time ago. He pulled the eyes out one time when I accidently lit one of his prized baseball cards on fire in an Easy-Bake Oven incident. Oops!"

She giggled just like you'd expect a little grade-school girl to giggle after telling a story in which she probably had committed arson. I think, anyway. I wasn't sure just what to expect anymore, honestly. And that's when I realized I had heard her voice before.

She looked up at me, and it was her. The too dark eyes. The face that looked way more innocent than what it concealed. I couldn't have forgotten this face. I'd seen it just a few months ago, after all.

"Holy, Blanton," I blurted out before I could stop myself. "You're Staples's sister!"

The weight of my sudden discovery clearly didn't hit her nearly as hard as it'd hit me. She just rubbed her ear and sighed, seeming uncomfortable for the first time.

"Oh, yeah, you're that kid who came to visit me last month with Barry, you and the taller, gangly one. You're like Barry's *little brothers*."

"Right," I said, not able to say much more at that moment due to shock.

"Yeah, Barry," she said, waving her hand as if to dismiss the whole thing like waving away a fly. "Barry used to think he was a big shot, and I guess I kinda did, too. I used to really look up to him. He had a cool business like this once. But where is he now? He visits me once every few weeks like that will suddenly make up for all these years of having abandoned me just like the rest of my family. Well I don't need him anymore, I can take care of myself. *Obviously*."

She didn't say any of this too bitterly or in a way that was asking for pity. She said it all as if merely stating facts. Things had occurred but now meant nothing. But I knew better.

"But he's changed, Abby," I said.

"Please, Mac," she said, "call me Kinko. Abby. Ugh, I *hate* that name, it's so dumb."

"Sorry, Kinko. . . . Wait, *Kinko*?"

"Yeah," she said, smirking. "That's what everyone who *really* knows me calls me."

So this was the rival businessman after all. I guess the name Ken-Co had come secondhand from Jimmy, so it wasn't surprising at all that he'd misheard or mispronounced it.

While I sat there in shock, she started writing something in a book in front of her. Probably taking notes like any good businessperson. But then after a few seconds I realized that she was coloring in a coloring book. She had an array of crayons in front of her, and the coloring book appeared to be of some cartoon about bratty-looking middle-school girls that I wasn't familiar with. She colored and then started humming. I glanced at her hired muscle, who was still motionless aside from his steady breathing. I couldn't tell for sure due to the sunglasses, but I was pretty sure he was staring right at me.

"Kinko, you need to listen to me. I swear that Staples has changed. He is really determined to get custody and take care of you."

"You idiot," she said.

I just looked at her.

"He hasn't changed. He just has you tricked again. He's been a screwup his whole life. Some people are just born that way. They can't, like, just change."

"I thought so too, but—"

Then I suddenly heard a kid screaming bloody murder somewhere faintly behind the door to our right. He was just screaming incoherently at first, but then was begging someone not to do something to him. From the sound of it I didn't even want to know what.

I looked at Kinko.

"Don't mind that. That's just some other business I was taking care of before you came here."

She started peeling stickers off a sheet of paper and sticking them into her coloring book while humming a song I recognized vaguely as belonging to one of the bands on the wall.

I didn't know what to say. The kid started screaming again. Kinko's strongman didn't react at all, as if whatever was happening behind that door was a frequent and usual occurrence. Then suddenly the door opened and the screaming was louder for just a second before another small girl emerged and closed the door behind her.

The girl was Asian, around the same age as Kinko, and wore all black to match her black hair. She smiled at Kinko. Then she walked over to the desk and whispered something into Kinko's ear.

Kinko laughed and nodded.

"Mark him," Kinko said without any hesitation.

The Asian girl nodded calmly and then exited through the same door. This time, in the brief moment the door was open, I heard the poor kid behind it clearly scream, "No! No, don't mark me, please. . . ." And then, just like that, the screams were once again reduced to faint background noise.

Kinko shook her head. "Sorry about that. That was my *assistant* Michi Oba. She, you know, takes care of the more difficult problems for me and stuff."

Just then the kid's screaming intensified momentarily,

and then it went silent. I tried again to swallow, again unsuccessfully.

"So, I heard a rumor that some nutty Shoobee was in the playground picking fights."

"Shoobee?"

She smirked at me like I was an idiot. "It's what we call outsiders, anybody who's obviously not from Thief Valley."

"Fair enough," I said. "The thing is I wasn't picking fights, though. The other kid started it."

I realized I likely sounded way more afraid of getting "marked" than I'd intended. Never let your fear show. Never show weakness.

"Well, that's, like, not the way I hear it, but that doesn't matter anyway. The point is I don't like Shoobees sneaking into my school at all, no matter what the reason."

As she said this, she ran a glue stick across her coloring book page. Then she sprinkled some loose sparkles and glitter across the glue trail. She raised the book and blew the excess glitter onto the floor. She examined her work and smiled widely.

"To be honest," I said, "I only broke in because I was trying to get a meeting with you."

She looked surprised for the first time. "With me?"

I nodded. "I'm assuming it was you who ordered the water balloon hit?"

"I didn't do it for you," Kinko said. "The Suits would have gotten their hands on you, then you'd be no good to me. I'd never have found out why, like, some random Shoobee broke into my school. And I don't like unsolved mysteries."

I nodded. I still didn't know what to say. I looked around at her mysterious underground lair, wondering how Staples's little sister could have gotten in the business this deep without anyone knowing about it. She was only a third grader, after all.

Kinko must have noticed me looking at the room because she said, "Pretty office, huh? Have you ever heard of Prohibition?"

"Uh . . ." I started, and then realized I had nowhere to go from there. I mean, it sounded vaguely familiar from school, but who remembers everything they learn? I really wished Vince were there with me in that moment.

Kinko smiled at me patiently. It wasn't the sort of smile that a third grader should have been able to give to a seventh grader.

"Well, I'll tell you about it, then!" she said with a laugh. "It was a long time ago, like, forever ago, when alcohol was illegal in America. You know what alcohol is, right? It's like beer and stuff that parents drink and it makes 'em, like, drunk and act stupid or whatever."

I nodded. Now she was just insulting me, but I didn't think she meant to. Either way, of course I knew what alcohol was.

"Anyway, people still wanted to drink it even though it was illegal. So tons of underground tunnels were built all across America, from New York City to Canada to Texas, even all the way up in North Dakota! They were built under schools, police stations, even under whole towns. And they were used to make and then smuggle booze all across the country so they have all kinds of, like, secret passages and hidden entrances and stuff."

"And these are some of those tunnels?" I said.

"Good for you!" she squealed. "You learn fast! Here, have a glitter star!"

She reached out and stuck a gold, glittery star sticker on the back of my hand, which had been resting on the desk. If this had come from an older kid, I might have taken this as a sarcastic insult, but she actually seemed to be pretty excited for me so I let it go. Besides, what was I going to do about it, fight a third-grade girl? I certainly wasn't going to try and last even half a round with her big sunglasses-wearing henchman.

"Anyway, enough small talk," she said loudly to show that we were going to get down to business. "Why did you come here to see me?"

# Chapter 22

## Jell-O and Fruit

I wanted to talk more about what she was thinking, getting involved in a business like this at her age, but decided to let it go for the time being. She clearly didn't want to talk about Staples, and I still had to solve the problem I came here about. It wouldn't have been a good idea to start the negotiation off with a stupid argument.

"Well, there's this kid who owes you money, apparently. Jimmy Two-Tone," I said.

Kinko laughed. "Oh, yeah, that guy! He makes me laugh."

I wanted to say, *"What doesn't make you laugh?"* but thought better of it.

"'Hey, Jimmy needs more time, dude!'" Kinko said,

doing a pretty good impression. Then she laughed again.

I laughed, too, this time figuring it couldn't hurt. The only one who didn't even crack a smile was old big-n-tall standing behind Kinko.

"So the point is I'd like to make good on his debt somehow. I want to square this thing with you, and I want out, for me, for Jimmy, for our entire school."

She smiled and nodded. "Oh, cool! Yeah, that sounds awesome. Where's the money? I can send someone over to pick it up, or do you have it with you?"

I shifted in my seat. "Well, that's the thing. I'd like to make good on the debt in another way. We don't have that kind of money. Like, maybe I could work for you for a while or something? I'm pretty okay at this kind of stuff."

She didn't say anything right away. Instead she started coloring the next picture in her book. She acted as if she hadn't even heard me. I glanced at the giant mook of a kid behind her, and he still stood there stone-faced. Was she about to snap and have me "marked" by Michi Oba? Was she thinking about it?

"I like you," she said suddenly. "You seem like a pretty cool kid. For a Shoobee."

"Thanks?"

"What I mean is," she continued without looking up, "$4,334.21 is a lot of money. The kind of money where, like, no matter how much I like you and stuff, you don't get out of it without paying. *Capiche?*"

I didn't know what exactly *"capiche"* meant, but that didn't matter; the rest of it had been pretty clear. Besides, I'd heard that word used in some of my favorite gangster movies before so it was pretty cool that she'd picked it up, too.

"You know, where I come from, sometimes favors and services can be worth just as much as money," I said. "Sometimes worth even more than money."

She finally looked up and put down her crayons. She took out some little hair piece thing and started fiddling with her hair, looking for a way to secure it with the little feather hair clip or whatever it's called.

"This isn't where you come from, though, is it?" she asked, finally settling on a place for the hair clip. She took out a little portable mirror to examine her hair.

"Uh, well, no, but, I mean . . ." I fumbled.

She just smiled and then shrugged. "So here's the deal. I do like you guys. You and Jimmy Two-Tone are two pretty funny fellas. So what I'll do is knock the amount down to an even four thousand dollars if you can pay it back to me in exactly one week. How's that?"

It was pretty fair, actually. I mean, aside from the fact that rounding up four thousand dollars in less than a week was impossible. But at this point it was all I had.

"Can you make it five weeks instead?"

"I don't negotiate," she said.

"Okay, one week. What about twenty-five hundred dollars?"

"I don't negotiate."

I looked at her blankly. I guessed I was lucky to have gotten a deal at all, even if it was one that we couldn't possibly deliver on.

"Isn't that right, Sue?" Kinko asked over her shoulder. "I don't negotiate, do I?"

"Sue?" I said in disbelief. That behemoth's name was Sue?

Kinko laughed. "Yeah, apparently his dad was really into this old singer named Jimmy Cash or something, and he has this song about, like, where this dude names his son Sue so that he'll have to fight a lot and be tough to survive or something. Pretty funny."

I looked at Sue. He didn't seem amused. But then he didn't seem angry either. He hadn't reacted at all to the question or us talking about his name.

"He doesn't talk much," Kinko explained with a shrug. "But he's a good guy. Right, Sue?"

No reaction.

"See?" Kinko said to me with a grin.

"Okay," I said. "Four grand, one week."

I held out my hand. She looked at it and hesitated.

"Well, there is one more little thing I'll need you to do for me as well. A job of sorts," she said.

"What sort of job?"

"I want to own your school," she said.

What was I supposed to say to that? Nothing, right? So I just laughed. Kinko laughed, too.

"Okay, so not, like, literally or whatever. But I want to own everyone there. I want their information, their addresses, grades, disciplinary records, everything. I want you to get me the permanent records of every kid in your school. Electronically, of course, on a flash drive."

Honestly, getting her the lease to the school might have actually been easier. I was starting to think Staples's little sister might be insane.

"I don't think . . ." I started.

"Listen, Mac, you can do it. Want to know how I know? Because I could do it here, no problem. You're supposed to be good, right? Well, then prove it. If I can take care of not only myself but also every kid in this school all by myself, then I bet you can do this one little task for me, right?"

"What are you going to use it for? I'm not here to get my school out of trouble only to see you mess around with it again."

"That's my business. I give you my word, though, that

none of your classmates will suffer. At least, not the ones who don't deserve it."

I opened my mouth to protest, but I realized I didn't have any other options. We were this deep, there wasn't any other way out of it. I held out my hand once again.

She shook it, and I suddenly couldn't believe I had just made a four-thousand-dollar deal with someone with such small hands.

"Do you like fruit in Jell-O?" she asked.

"Um . . . I don't know. No, I guess not," I said.

"I think it's gross," she said, making a face. "Our school cafeteria puts fruit in the Jell-O here. It's *so* nasty!"

I just sat there, completely dumbstruck.

"Okay, I have business to do," she said. "I'll have the Aussie escort you off school property using the tunnels so you don't get caught."

"Thanks," I said, getting up to leave.

"One last thing before you go."

I turned back. "Yeah?"

"Not one penny less, one missing permanent record, or one day late or all of those little tiny things we've done to your school will seem like carnival games compared to what we'll do next."

I nodded and once again failed at an attempt to swallow saliva that was basically nonexistent.

The Aussie was waiting for me in the main chamber. He greeted me with a giant lopsided smile.

"Hey, mate, you're still alive! That's good to see. And you didn't even get marked. See? I told you it would all come out good!"

"How did it go?" Staples asked as I got into his car.

"Fine," I said.

"So what's this Ken-Co guy like anyway?"

I took a deep breath. I thought about telling him, *"Oh, well, you know she's okay, considering she's as smart and shrewd and psychotic as you are, which I guess isn't surprising considering it's your sister."* But the moment I thought about that, I had a vision of him snapping and punching me repeatedly in the face for bringing him such bad news.

"He's smart," I said. "We were able to make a deal at least."

I decided not to tell him just yet. I mean, if he knew his sister was making all the same mistakes he did, that she was following the same path, it might just kill him. Or send him over the edge. Either one would likely end poorly for both him and me.

On the drive back I told him all about the deal we'd made. At the end he glanced at me and then said, "Well, let's just hope you're as good as you think you are."

# Chapter 23

## Impossible

"**B**ut that's impossible!" Vince yelled. Not at me, of course, just the situation. "Four grand in a week. I mean, we've never even come close to making *one* thousand in a week. Not even in our best ones! Plus, every kid's permanent record? I mean, we've never been able to crack that even without the Suits on our tails."

"I know, Vince," I conceded. "What other options did I have?"

He thought about this and then shrugged and plopped down onto the chair next to the desk in my room. Vince had come over as soon as his mom had gotten home from work and let him leave the house. It had taken me a while to explain my day because Vince kept asking so many questions. And I could hardly blame him. I mean, hearing the story come out of my own mouth made me realize just how surreal my day had been.

"And you're sure Staples doesn't know?" he asked.

I shook my head. "It sure didn't seem like it."

Vince nodded. "Well, he is basically a professional liar."

"He can't know about his sister's involvement. He would have said something to us. There'd be no benefit to him keeping it a secret."

"What benefit is there from us keeping it a secret from him?" Vince asked.

I shrugged. "I was afraid he'd kill the messenger. After all, her running a giant crime ring was exactly what he'd said he didn't want."

"Shoot the messenger," Vince said.

"Huh?"

"Never mind. So what are we going to do, then?" Vince asked. "I mean, we have only like a little over a thousand dollars of our old Funds left. Assuming we even want to just donate all of our money to this mess, that still leaves us with around three thousand dollars to go!"

"We'll do the only thing we can do: earn the money and then pay back Kinko," I said calmly. Even now a plan was brewing.

"But how?" Vince asked, pivoting the chair back and forth so that the sides hit my desk over and over in rhythm. "And what about the permanent records?"

"We'll call in every outstanding favor owed to us. Round up all of our former employees. We'll open up business again. Take donations. Put together a network of legitimate lemonade stands while it's still hot outside, which is a market we should have tapped into years ago. Basically we'll put together the most massive operation we ever have. It will be a whole empire squeezed into one week. I don't know yet about the permanent records, but we'll come up with something, right? We always do."

Vince nodded slowly. I could see he was catching on to the thought that this just might work. That wasn't surprising; he was a genius, after all.

"Yeah," he said, "we could also do bake sales during lunch, sell our old video games, arrange fights between bullies and sell tickets! We can even get our hands on the newest R-rated movies and M-rated video games and sell them at a markup to kids who aren't allowed to get them."

"Now you're talking. That's genius! We'll do anything, everything we can. What have we got to lose?" I said.

"There is one major flaw to this plan, though, not to mention the dozens of smaller ones," Vince said, being his usual logical self.

"What's that?" I asked, even though I knew what he was going to say.

"The Suits: they'll sniff us out in no time. We've got no chance to avoid detection with such a massive amount of stuff we'll be in charge of. And as you know, the permanent records are located in the administration offices. So there's that."

"Oh, that," I said. "We don't need to worry about the Suits for now. For that problem I've got a plan. It's probably the most insane plan I've ever had, but I think it just might work."

# Chapter 24

## Operation Chaos

The next morning at recess I made the spot behind the Shed the most dangerous place in the school. Only one other time before had our school seen such an epic gathering of bullies, punks, tough kids, and psychos. And I had been responsible for that incident as well. I was starting to feel like I was kind of like the school's favorite potato chips. Like, on the surface I was awesome and the school loved me, but in the end too much of me would eventually kill it.

But, anyways, both meetings of bullies felt necessary in their own way at the time. Except that this time I had to arrange the meeting much more secretively. The first thing I did at school that morning was to find Ears.

Ears was the best gossiper in the school now that Prep-School had transferred to some private academy a few hours away.

I told him to start a rumor that any bully or tough kid or anybody who just generally loved wreaking havoc should show up behind the Shed at the start of early recess. Anybody who came would get five dollars just for showing up.

It didn't take long for Ears's handiwork to pay off. By my second class that day I had overheard a few kids talking about it in the hallway. Sometimes you had to love the power of the Werk. The Werk was the name given to our school's web of gossip and rumors. You know, as in "network." Why they'd decided to spell it with an E is a mystery, even to me. With gossips you never really can know for sure why they say or do anything that they do.

Anyways, at early recess that morning, the crowd of bullies that gathered was pretty impressive. In attendance were all of my occasional employees like Nubby, Great White, Little Paul, Kevin, Kitten, Snapper, and iBully, as well as several other bullies who I'd never worked with before.

Like Spitball Chad. Spitball Chad was this strange kid with curly red hair and ears that were small but still poked out of his hair like little antennae. It kind of made him look like a wombat. Anyways, as you might guess, Spitball Chad was known for always sitting in the back of the classroom and shooting spitballs at kids. He even had different-sized straws for different calibers of spitballs. His were especially soggy, too, which was as disgusting as it sounded. He always seemed to have saliva crusted around the corners of his mouth like dried frosting or something. Needless to say, we all assumed Spitball Chad would never find a girlfriend on account of being just kind of gross.

Then there was Dead Bolt, a fifth grader with a lightning bolt shaved into the side of his head. He was a big kid and pretty intimidating, but that's all he had. He was all talk and no walk, if you know what I mean. But the thing was most kids didn't know better. So when he threatened them, they just gave in and gave him their lunch money or whatever it was he was bullying them for. If anyone were ever to stand up to him, he always backed down.

Near the back of the crowd of kids was the Mantis. He was an eighth grader but was already like six feet five inches tall. The problem was that he weighed only like ninety pounds. Seriously, he was all angles. But he always had the leverage on you. And he was as mean as he was skinny. One time I had seen him using two fourth graders as crutches just for the heck of it. His signature move, though, was stealing kids' backpacks and shoes and cell phones and then sticking them in the rain gutters along the roof of the portables where no one else could reach them.

I passed out the five-dollar bills to everyone in attendance. Dead Bolt took his cash and started to walk away. I was annoyed, but this had been expected. I figured some kids would show just for the cash and then take off. I was actually pretty pleased that he was the only one.

But Great White charged after him.

"Hey, where do ya think you're running off to, ya git?" he said in his awesome British accent.

Dead Bolt turned and sized him up.

"I got what I came here for."

"My chum here paid you that money for a spot of your time. Now you're going to listen to him or I'll have to take that fiver back and keep it for myself."

Great White got right in his face. They were about the same height, but Dead Bolt easily had a good thirty pounds on him. I really did appreciate the gesture, especially coming from a kid like Great White who had never shown himself to be particularly chivalrous, but the last thing I needed was for a fight to break out. If one punch got thrown in front of a crowd like this, we'd have a full-scale prison-grade riot on our hands in less than thirty seconds.

Dead Bolt made a quick motion toward Great White as if trying to scare him, trying to get him to flinch. But Great White didn't budge an inch. Instead he smirked.

"That it?" he asked.

Dead Bolt paused, and for a second I didn't think he would back down. I could have smacked myself for being so reckless. Holding this kind of meeting was like taking a bath in a tub full of unstable sticks of dynamite.

But then Dead Bolt, true to form, shook his head and started walking back to the group.

"Fine. I'll listen to his stupid speech thing or whatever. But I'm keeping the money."

Great White nodded, and they both rejoined the lineup and everybody turned back toward me. I started by taking out a roll of twenties, just like I had a year ago in the East Wing boys' bathroom.

They gathered around a little closer, their eyes wide like those of a pack of feral lions picking up the scent of blood in the air.

"How would you all like to get paid to wreak some havoc?" I asked.

The expected ripple of excitement passed, and then Great White, who I'd hired for a similar job a year ago asked, "Who are we targeting this time?"

"This time," I said, "there is no target. I just need you all to create chaos here. Pull fire alarms, get into fights, pull pranks, graffiti the place, anything and everything you can do to get the full attention of the Suits. I want you to keep the principal so busy that he doesn't even have time to eat lunch every day."

This time it was more than just a ripple. This time the group of bullies almost cheered like they were at a football game. I saw excited and scary grins as well as some knuckle-cracking.

"And definitely play to your strengths," I continued. "Like you, iBully. Don't feel like you need to try and get into fights. Instead, you should hack the school mainframe. Delete important school files, kids' grade reports, attendance reports, whatever. Turn the school network into a piece of Swiss cheese."

"What's in this for you?" Little Paul asked, not even trying to hide his suspicion.

"I just need the Suits' attention off of me while I try to make some money this week. It's for a good cause."

"How much will we get paid?" Nubby asked. "I mean, we'll get detention for this stuff, probably a lot of it. Maybe even suspended."

A few other bullies nodded in agreement.

"For one, most of you already get detention every week anyway, right? You might as well earn some free cash while you're at it."

Many of them nodded reluctantly and grinned. Most

bullies were proud of how much detention they got. Like, the more time served, the more bully-cred it earned you. Reputation was everything.

"But," I continued, "you get two dollars for every confirmed distraction you create. That might not seem like a lot, but I'm paying you guys to do what you love to do. Stuff that you'll probably do anyway, eventually."

I would've added that they would also be helping out the school and all the kids here in a major way, but this was probably the one crowd on which that argument was likely to backfire.

"When do we start?" Kitten asked.

Kitten was calm, quiet as usual. He normally almost never talked unless it was absolutely necessary. But beneath the calm question, I could see what was driving it; this was a dream assignment for him. He couldn't wait to unleash some frustration on this place.

"Right now," I said, and smiled. "Operation Chaos commences immediately."

# Chapter 25

## The Fourth Stall from the High Window

Once I was sure that the massive fight I had staged among the group of bullies was out of control enough that the principal as well as both recess supervisors would need to help break it up and sort it all out, I snuck away to the East Wing. I had an office to reclaim.

Vince stood at the end of the hallway to keep watch for teachers or Suits. Yeah, we'd staged a massive diversion in the form of the largest school yard brawl in school history, but just the same, we still had to be careful.

Mitch tried to stop me from cutting in the line, which wasn't nearly as long as it had been the last time I had been there. Word was obviously getting out that Jimmy

Two-Tone was starting to have problems following through.

"Wait, you can't just cut," Mitch started.

I shoved his hand aside and walked through the doorway into the bathroom before he even had a chance to react.

"Hey!" Justin said.

"I need to see Jimmy," I said.

"Well, he's busy." Justin stepped in front of me with his arms crossed.

I was starting to calculate places I could strike first to catch him offguard. Places where my first blow would incapacitate him enough that the fight would be over right then and there. Because I probably had no chance in a fight against Justin if it lasted much longer than that. But then Jimmy must have heard me.

"It's okay, Justin. Jimmy has been expecting this dude," Jimmy called out from the fourth stall from the high window.

Justin scowled at me, but he did step aside.

I entered the stall and sat down.

"Hey, Mac! Good to see you, bud," Jimmy said.

"Hey, Jimmy," I said. "So I talked to Kinko at Thief Valley Elementary."

"What did he say, bro?"

"Well, *she* agreed to let us pay her back at a reduced

rate, just as long as we do it within a week."

Jimmy made a face like I had just told him we had to clean the faculty bathroom toilet, which every kid in school knew was probably the grossest in the state.

"How are we going to do that? I mean . . ."

"I think we can get the money together, but I need a home base. An office from which to conduct the operation."

He nodded. "All right, you can have it back. But what about the Suits? Jimmy thought you couldn't come back here, dude?"

"Don't worry about the Suits. I've got that covered. I'm also going to want my own crew, as well. Can we move in during lunch?"

Jimmy nodded. "I think so, sure."

I reached out and shook his hand like you're supposed to after a business deal. Well, two things down, just about four hundred eighteen million to go.

And just like that, we were back in business. Despite all my efforts to retire, to walk away, here we were once again in the fourth stall from the high window, working to make money and solve problems. Of course, things were a little different than they had been the last time we'd been open for business at the end of the last school year. For one thing Joe was in high school now, so I had a new strongman.

Nubby was a pretty reasonable kid for a bully. A lot of his bullying came as a result of avoiding being teased over his stubby mallet of a right hand. So he wasn't particularly mean, but at the same time he was big and strong and had just enough of an edge to keep kids in line. Plus, he was pretty smart. So I hired Nubby as my new strongman.

Fred, who used to keep the office records for us, instead was positioned near the end of the hallway to watch out for Suits. So far the bullies had already done a great job keeping their hands full, but we had to be extra careful anyway. All it took was one bully to squeal on me, and Dickerson would be marching down this way first thing. I hired a kid named Tanzeem, who had helped me in the past, to watch the East Wing entrance near my office, in case the Suits tried to flank us.

Another major difference with our business this time was that we took customers in three at a time. In the past we had only let one customer in at a time. But now with Vince having his own desk station in the corner by the sink and Jimmy setting up under the high window along the far wall, we were able to pull triple duty. That's right. For the first time ever Vince would be taking customers on his own. He was nervous about it because dealing with the customers directly had never been his strong suit, but I was confident he'd be fine. After all, he was the smartest kid in the school, hands down.

It didn't matter anyway; we had no choice. We had too much money to make and too little time to do it to worry about such things. We just had to get to work.

The next order of business was to hire a kid named Huston to oversee the implementation of our new lemonade stand venture. Huston was a good kid, if not a little odd. Growing up, most kids dream of playing sports . . . well, he'd always dreamed of someday becoming a referee for a professional sports league. By second grade he'd started wearing these homemade referee uniforms, which were white T-shirts with crude vertical black strips drawn on them with markers. And he had his whistle, of course, which all during recess he'd blow and then try to call penalties on kids for "unnecessary roughness on the teeter-totter, cherry bump with too much force" or "traveling, too much speed down the slide" or "illegal contact" when this one kid tried to playfully hug a girl that Huston had a crush on.

Anyways, he was perfect for the lemonade stand enterprise since it was a pretty large operation and it needed the leadership of someone who loved to order people around and could stick to a list of rules. They'd set up the stands behind the Shed and behind the skating rink warming house on school property during school hours. And then more stands would be all over the neighborhood in the early evenings and that week-end. Our business model would be simple: fresh, cold, quality lemonade, a premium product for a premium price. People would pay for quality.

Before Huston left my office that day at lunch, dur-ing which time we'd discussed business and drawn up the plans for the lemonade operation and everything, he blew his whistle.

"Unsportsmanlike conduct!" he shouted. "Number Mac of the offense. Being too good a businessman for the competition."

At this he laughed uncontrollably. My guess was that if other umpires or referees would have been there, they'd have laughed, too. As for me, well, I politely faked it. Lame referee humor wasn't my thing, but I didn't want to insult my new Lemonade Stand Manager.

The next kid Nubby ushered into my office that day was the first regular customer of the day. Which made him the first postretirement customer of my career. And he turned out to be the sort of wacko that had partially pushed me into retirement in the first place.

He entered the stall and right away I smelled it. The smell of burned toast, or burned pizza, or camping. The smell of fire. His hands were black and dirty with soot, and one of his eyebrows was missing, presumably from some sort of fire mishap. A single match stuck out from the corner of his mouth like a toothpick.

"Have a seat," I said to the kid, who was fidgeting nervously with an empty matchbox.

He sat down.

"Name?"

"People call me Matches," he said.

"What can I do for you, Matches?" I asked, making notes in my Books.

"I want this new video game, but I can't get it because it's rated M and my parents won't let me get it."

"Yeah, we got you covered, no problem," I said. This was a pretty routine request. Easy money. "We'll need cash up front for the game itself plus a twenty-five-percent service charge for acquiring the game for you. Does that sound good?"

Matches nodded and pulled out a wad of crumpled cash. I never understood why so many kids kept their money balled up into little piles, but over the years I'd gotten used to it.

"Great," I said, counting out the necessary cash. "Do you want to pick up the game here? Or do you want to pay another three dollars for locker-side delivery?"

"Delivery," Matches said, practically salivating.

"Okay, what game title and platform are we getting for you?" I asked, stacking the money neatly on my desk and then making notes in my Books.

"It's called *Arsonist*," he said. "I need it on Xbox 360."

I stopped writing and gave him a look. Seriously? He just grinned at me, the match dancing on the corner of his lip.

"I'm afraid to even ask what the game is about," I said.

"Basically, you're this arsonist, right? And it's an open-world format game like *GTA* or *Fallout*. So you just go around this city and set stuff on fire and then collect more tools of the trade along the way so you can set even bigger fires. And then, once you start burning buildings, you get bonus points for the more people that are inside them."

"That's the sickest thing I've ever heard," I said simply. I didn't think much more needed to be said.

"What?" Matches laughed. "You sound like my mom. I know the people aren't real! It's just a game."

I shook my head. "All right, whatever, Matches. We'll deliver it to you Friday."

He grinned again and got up. I watched the psycho leave, making sure he wasn't going to start my office on fire on the way out. Man, kids these days. I mean, I liked FPS and war games as much as the next guy, especially for multiplayer, but that game sounded like it was taking it a little too far. Then again, considering the things I'd seen and witnessed the past year while running my business, maybe that game wasn't all that ridiculous after all.

Part of me even considered hiring Matches. I mean, a kid like that could cause some massive diversions to attract the Suits' attention. But then my common sense got the better of me. I mean, there was a limit to the kind of activities I would let myself fund; I had to draw the line *somewhere*.

So for the rest of that day we worked as hard as we ever had before. And with us pulling in three times the amount of customers as usual, we made a record profit. So we were off to a good start. But there was just one little problem: I still had no idea how to get the permanent records.

The next day at morning recess I met up with iBully in my office. I told him what I needed. He could hack into anything, so I was convinced he could get me into the school's servers. But turns out I was wrong.

"No can do," he said.

"Why not? I thought you could hack into anything within the school's network?"

"Well, for one, there are a huge number of files. I don't think I could get enough uninterrupted time in the school's mainframe to download them all to my computer to save them to a drive. And also, they're kept on a separate server than everything else. They're only on the district's server, which can only be accessed through Dickerson's computer."

I nodded. "No problem. We'll break into his office at night. We've done it before, broken into a principal's office. Easy."

iBully shook his head again. "No, that won't work either. It'd be way too detectable and traceable, for one, because he will know he wasn't at his computer at night. And two, the system that houses the records shuts down for backup and program updates every evening. If we try to get the files once that process has started, we could crash the whole system and erase the files. No, the only way I could get them for you is if you got me into his office in the middle of the day for close to an hour without any interruptions."

I sat back in my chair and sighed. That would be impossible. I mean, with the amount of bullies getting in trouble, Dickerson was spending tons of time in his office disciplining them, calling parents, and crying in frustration, probably.

"Okay," I said. "We'll figure something out. I'll be in touch."

I slid a five across my desk for his time. iBully picked it up and left.

At afternoon recess Vince and I took a quick break to discuss a few cases before we let in the first few customers. So far Vince had done pretty well for himself.

Not that I was surprised. He knew the business as well as I did; he only thought he didn't.

It was nice to take a quick break to catch up. We'd been working nonstop for two days. The night before, we'd spent the whole evening helping to get the lemonade stands set up so they'd be ready for business after school the next day. We were even going to stock them with Rice Krispie treats. I couldn't believe how much money could be made on those. They were so cheap to make, especially when parents were footing the bill for ingredients.

So it had been a busy evening. Vince and I had even established a new after-hours office in the playground behind his trailer. The same playground that we'd first built our business in. We were open every night from five to seven thirty and had been telling kids all day to spread the word, not just to kids around here but to their friends and family at other schools, in other towns. Anybody who needed help could come and get it for a fee behind the slide in Vince's trailer park playground.

"So, ready for the ultimate trivia challenge?" Vince asked me after we'd finished discussing our cases.

"Actually, I think I'll pass," I said. "We just can't waste any time right now."

Vince made a face, but he knew I was right. He eventually nodded and grinned.

"Yeah, it's like my grandma always says, 'If there's work to be done, then there's no point to stuffing your pockets full of feathers because, after all, a spaceship is only as heavy as the talking goats that are driving it, unless of course they're transporting gold. Then it's even heavier. And tastier.'"

I laughed. Which was nice to do. I hadn't even taken a break long enough to laugh since my meeting with Kinko a few days before.

"You mean she actually manages to say all of that without passing out?"

Vince shrugged. "She's amazing, what can I say? There's actually even more to it, but I condensed it to save time."

I couldn't argue with that. And so we went back to our desks in separate corners of the bathroom and signaled to Nubby to start letting the customers in. There was much work still to be done.

# Chapter 26

## The Mac-Franchise

We were pulling out all the stops. I mean, we had to. We had no chance of reaching our goal if we didn't do anything and everything we could think of to make money. My first customer that night during our after-school office hours in the trailer park playground was proof of that. He was an old friend and former employee who didn't even go to our school anymore.

"Hey, Joe," I said.

"Hey, Mac," he said with a huge smile. "I heard you wanted to see me?"

"That's right," I said. "I'm glad word got to you."

"What's going on? How's the old school? High school is awesome, by the way. You and Vince are going to love it."

We chatted a little while about how his year was going, and then I filled Joe in on the situation. I left nothing out. Besides Vince, Joe had been my oldest and most trusted employee for the past four years.

"Man, that's a pickle," he said.

I nodded.

"But how can I help?"

"Spread the word. I mean, I know high school kids might scoff at coming to a seventh grader for help, but I have to think they have just as many problems, if not more, than we do, right?"

Joe thought this over and then nodded. "Yeah, well, I don't know if they do have more problems, but they definitely complain about everything more."

"Right. So spread the word. You can act as the business front there. We'll even split profits with you. You take customers, bring their problems to me, we'll fix them, and then get back to you. Or tell you how to fix them. Anything they need, we can help them."

Joe took a long time to mull it over. Which was fine. If he was in, I wanted him to be sure. Eventually he did what I knew he would. You can always count on guys like Joe to do the right thing.

"Okay, I'm in," he said. "I'll see if I can drum up any business at the high school."

"Perfect," I said. "Just meet me here every night at

six and we'll go over your business dealings. I never thought I'd end up having someone open a franchise."

Joe laughed and then stood to leave. "Before I go, though, could I hear one grandma quote, you know, just for old time's?"

I looked at Vince, who was grinning from ear to ear. Nothing made him happier than getting requests for grandma quotes. Well, okay, maybe Cubs victories made him happier, but grandma-quote requests were definitely a close second.

"Joe, my grandma always says, 'Let no sapphires of the Bombay variety go to waste, lest you want to end up inside a closet crying and wearing a Richard Nixon mask while your grandpa tries to feed applesauce to the lamp in the living room.'"

Joe burst out laughing and then clapped Vince on the shoulder in a friendly way. He waved good-bye to me while still chuckling and then hopped on his bike and rode off. I signaled to Nubby to let the next customer through.

It was Staples. And he had brought a guest.

Kinko.

"Hey, Mac," Staples said. "I came to check in on things."

At first I thought Kinko had told him something. But clearly she didn't, since Staples hadn't pounded me into eel food. Staples had been filled in on all of our operations and had even been helping when he could. Delivering supplies to lemonade stands in his car, buying us various movies and video games that we wouldn't have been allowed to due to our age, stuff like that.

"Good," I said, eyeing Kinko warily. She just sat there next to Staples and grinned at me.

"Isn't this great? Her jerk foster parents let her come with for once; we're going to a movie," Staples said.

He was beaming. His sister had finally agreed to let him treat her to something fun. But I knew it was an act. She had probably agreed to go with him solely to spy on me.

"Hi," she said. "I'm Abby."

"Yeah, we, uh, met at your school several weeks ago near the playground . . . remember?" I said.

She shook her head, still grinning at me. The most evil smile imaginable.

This was awkward.

"So there are kids at our school talking all about your school," she said.

"Oh yeah?" I played along.

"Yeah! I guess there's this kid, Mac, who goes here who owes a ton of money to this guy at our school named Kinko. And kids are saying that Mac's really gonna get it if he doesn't come through. I mean, Kinko is pretty psycho. Nobody crosses Kinko."

I swallowed. Or tried to.

"See?" Staples said. "Listen to that! Her school is messed-up. We have to fix this."

"Yeah, fix this!" Kinko said, and then giggled, pretending that she had no idea what Staples meant.

I nodded.

"Boy, I sure do feel bad for this Mac kid, though," she said. "They said he's running out of time. The kids at my school are crazeeeeeee. Just for a kid sneezing too loud they'll, like, steal his shoes and start them on fire and melt them down into a puddle of rubbery goo and then make the kid's dog eat it all! Crazy, huh?"

Staples nodded. "I told you Thief Valley was rough. Anyway, let's go. The show starts soon."

He reached out for Kinko's hand, but she ignored it. Instead she got up, wiped her face with her sleeve, and winked at me.

Staples gave up and put his hands in his pockets and started walking back toward his car with Kinko walking next to him. She turned back toward me and drew her index finger across her throat while smiling, then started skipping out ahead of Staples toward his car.

I looked at Vince, and he was almost white like a ghost. I then realized that had been his first in-person glimpse of how truly diabolical that little third-grade girl could be. I cleared my throat and motioned for Nubby to usher over the next customer.

It was a young girl, maybe first grade. She was bawling and had snot running down her dirty face. I sighed and glanced at Vince, who managed a smirk. Sometimes working could actually be kind of fun, and other times it was, well, work. I put on a fake smile and greeted the wailing first grader, deciding that she likely wouldn't be able to even pay me enough to be worth the time. But if I was going to do this, I was going to do it right, which still meant not turning away customers, no matter how small or poor or snot-faced they were.

# Chapter 27

## One Day Left

That weekend was huge for us. We had more operations and business ventures running that weekend than we'd ever had before times ten. We had a movie and video game booth set up selling dozens of the newest R- and M-rated titles. We had a test answer and homework blowout, for which Vince and I amassed all of the essay papers, book reports, work sheet packets, and test answer keys we'd collected over the years into one giant file cabinet. We priced all the items and put them up for sale at bargain prices. And they sold like we were selling gold for pocket lint. But then, why wouldn't they? What kid wouldn't want to buy enough prewritten essay papers to last him a whole school year for a mere fifty dollars?

Other things we had going that weekend were the lemonade stand and conjoined baked good/dessert stands. Lots of kids helping us had asked their moms and dads for treats and then they smuggled them out of the house and sold them to us for cheap. We turned around and sold them for slightly more to other kids. You'd think that that might be kind of a lame business, but with so many parents freaking out about eating healthy these days, you'd be surprised at just how many kids were treat-deprived and desperate to pay for a good old-fashioned chocolate chip cookie or brownie.

Plus, we were just lucky enough to have the hottest weekend of the fall, with temperatures getting up and over one hundred degrees on Saturday and Sunday. And since it was projected to be one of the last nice weekends of the year, everybody was outside trying to take advantage. All of that added up to record profits from the lemonade stands, which Huston ran with an iron fist. And lots of whistle blowing and penalties, such as "illegal use of hands" (for touching the cookies without gloves) or "personal foul" (for trying to embezzle a few bucks from the afternoon sales).

Joe also came through with some business for us from high school kids. Not as much as I felt was possible, but still enough to generate a few hundred dollars of business. And in this predicament literally every last cent would help.

We also got some visits from kids we didn't know from nearby towns. I guessed word had really spread. Many of those kids were starving for this type of help, so out-of-towners and kids from other schools in town really drove up the movie and video game sales.

Even Staples had found more ways to help out. Some kids offered to pay for pictures with the old crime legend. Sure, I'd taken him down a year ago, but for many kids that didn't erase the name he'd built for himself. He was still a living legend. And disappearing like he had after our showdown last year only heightened his mysterious and legendary status in some kids' minds.

Tyrell agreed to partner with me as well and offered his spy services on a freelance basis to kids. He split profits with me 50/50, and there were a surprising number of kids who hired him to do some spying for them.

Between all of our new branches at the high school, in the lemonade business, etc., and pulling triple shifts between Vince, Jimmy Two-Tone, and me, we were doing pretty well. And by doing pretty well, I mean we were taking in boatloads of cash.

Of course it wasn't all profit. In my economics class that year we'd learned about the difference between gross income and net income, and I don't want to bore you with specifics, but let's just say all the money you make isn't always direct profit that you get to keep.

This size operation called for a lot of employees. Employees who had to be paid, though many of them were working for a discount. We had to pay helpers, pay for the goods sold, pay for bully protection and bully diversions. And I had to say, they had done a pretty good job keeping the Suits so distracted that they had no idea what I was up to.

Some of the confirmed diversions I'd heard about included a fight between Little Paul and a pack of third graders that spanned the whole length of the football field and involved raw eggs, a wad of chewed gum, and a bottle of hand sanitizer. Also, Kitten had been on his game, at one point threatening a teacher with a water balloon filled with iodine. He even got a few days of in-school suspension for that one.

Other notable incidents included the school sprin-kler system being set off not once, not twice, but four times; the return of the Graffiti Ninja, albeit a less talented version; and iBully supposedly planting some small bugs into the school's network. As of right now, the internet home page for every computer in the whole building was stuck as this website called www.gerbilpoop.com, which is this gross site that probably doesn't need further explanation. And the school computer guy still hadn't been able to fix it. All in all, the school was a chaotic mess.

Which, yeah, I knew was a little risky considering what had happened last year with Dr. George and almost having the school shut down. But this time was different. This time there was no massive test failure to serve as the linchpin. This time it was just a culmination of petty acts of vandalism and sabotage. It was kind of funny, in a way, that we were sabotaging our own school in order to avoid worse sabotage from an outside source. It barely made sense if any at all. But like Staples said, you can't get out without making sacrifices.

Normally I'm not the sort of guy who likes to brag about myself. But even I had to admit that we were at the top of our game. Our business had never functioned better, had never made more money. By Monday morning it somehow seemed like we actually might achieve the impossible and be able to pay back Kinko on Tuesday.

The biggest problem still at hand, of course, was that we had only one day left to get the permanent records. Which is why Sunday night I had called a special meeting with Vince and several select kids. We came up with probably our most insane and complicated plan ever.

# Chapter 28

## Erasing the Line Previously Drawn

Have you ever seen a movie or TV program that shows the stock market? Not like the scrolling thing on the bottom of the screen on news channels with a bunch of numbers and symbols. I mean, like footage of something called the stock exchange floor. Well, if you haven't, basically it's a bunch of people wearing dress shirts and suits running around with papers in their hands, waving and screaming and climbing all over one another.

If there was such a thing as a video dictionary and you looked up the word "chaos," the definition would be footage from the stock market exchange floor. One time I caught my dad watching some news show on CNN where they were talking about the stock market and they were showing footage of the exchange floor that day. It was madness; I swore I even saw one guy standing on a desk holding a live chicken. He was threatening to douse the chicken with a glass of water while doing some sort of weird barefoot dance. And two other guys in the background were on the ground wrestling, and I saw one of them bite the other one in the cheek. And that's not even mentioning the dude in the panda suit who was starting small fires near the elevators in the background and then putting them out with two-liter bottles of Pepsi.

Anyways, the point is that was exactly the atmosphere of our office that Monday.

There were kids piling in during every recess and all during lunch. Vince and I were in overdrive mode trying to get through enough business to hit our goal, but we knew that the number was within reach. All either of us could think about was later that day, stealing the permanent records.

The main obstacle we faced would be, of course, getting all three secretaries and Dickerson out of the administration offices for at least a full hour at the same time. Something that had never happened before during a school day. In fact, the only time they were ever even out of the office at the same time at all was during fire drills, but that was usually just for like ten minutes at the most. And iBully was adamant that he needed at least an hour.

But luckily, we had Vince. And he had come up with one of the most brilliant plans either of us had ever concocted.

Stage one was for me, Vince, and iBully to head to the library, which was adjacent to the administration offices, where we could watch the plan unfold without looking too suspicious. The plan was for no one else to enter the offices but us three and Tyrell, who insisted on finding his own observation point. If any of us was caught, it would obviously be instant expulsion, so I didn't want any more kids involved than were absolutely necessary.

I checked my watch; stage two should be starting at any moment.

Sure enough, after about ten more seconds, Dickerson came exploding out of the administration offices. He turned down the hall, walking in that stiff way adults do when they need to move quickly but don't want to run. Then after a few steps he gave up and just took off running.

So he'd clearly seen his car getting towed. I knew from all the time I'd spent in his office the past year that he sat facing the window and that his parking space was right there, the one directly across from the window.

Getting a car towed was actually pretty easy. We just had My-Me call the towing company pretending to be Mr. Dickerson complaining that an unauthorized vehicle was parked in his spot. The tow company obviously would have no idea that they were actually towing Dickerson's car. The way towers work is they get a call for a tow, they make the tow. They run a simple business, which means they don't ask questions; they just make money.

As soon as we saw Dickerson run out the door at the end of the hall, it meant phase three should already be under way. So Vince, iBully, and I left the library and went to the nearest boys' bathroom just down the hall. We each occupied a stall and stood on the toilet, waiting for the chaos to begin.

By then Matches should have already started his fire just outside the cafeteria windows. I know, I know. I said there was a line and that I'd never actually pay a kid to set our school on fire and blah, blah, blah. But the thing is, desperate times call for crazy stuff to happen.

Just pulling the fire alarm would clear the building for only fifteen minutes maximum. But a real fire would clear it for at least forty-five minutes, maybe even for the whole day. Or so I hoped . . . If I was wrong, our plan was doomed.

You might be wondering why we had Dickerson's car towed when the fire thing would work to clear out everybody. Well, the thing is Dickerson's job when there was a fire was to keep sweeping the building for any kids left behind. So, this way, if he was distracted with the tow-truck guys, he wouldn't be able to do that. Or so I could only hope.

Anyways, we didn't have to wait long before we heard the fire alarm. Matches assured me that he could start a fire big enough to cause a panic, yet one that would stay reasonably under control. I hoped he was right. If the fire spread inside, the four of us would all get cooked like holiday hams.

We waited in the bathroom, standing on the toilets. Pretty soon the door burst open and a teacher made a pass-through, checking for any kids who might have been in there. He got down on his knees to check for feet and then was gone. We waited for five more minutes to make sure the school was cleared and then we made our move.

Out in the hallway we could smell smoke. I was suddenly very concerned that Matches had started a fire that would actually burn the whole place down. I shook it off and joined Tyrell at the door to the administration offices. He was already working on the lock with his trusty lockpick gun.

In just a matter of minutes he had us inside the administrative office area and then a short time later into Dickerson's actual office. We stayed low so we wouldn't be seen by everyone outside.

"Okay, do your thing," I said to iBully.

He sat down at Dickerson's desk, making sure to stay hidden right behind the monitor. He plugged a flash drive into the computer and started clacking away at the keyboard.

I poked my head up just enough to see outside. There were throngs of kids milling around, laughing and joking. Teachers doing head counts. And Dickerson was still out there simultaneously arguing with the tow-truck driver while trying to deal with the mess of his school being on fire. I saw two fire trucks coming up quickly from down the street.

I slid back down and looked at Vince. Now all we could do was wait and hope that it took the firefighters a while to get everything under control.

After what felt like forever but was only a little over half an hour, iBully finally said, "Almost done. I just need like ten more minutes."

I grinned at Vince. We were actually going to pull this off. I didn't believe it. But then Tyrell, who had been keeping watch in the hallway, poked his head inside the office.

"Uh, guys, Dickerson is coming! The fire chief must have let him back in for something. ETA like seventy seconds."

# Chapter 29

## The Ultimate Sacrifice

**V**ince and I looked at each other. Everything else around us stopped. We'd gotten so close to pulling it off that it actually hurt to finally lose like this. It was like the 2003 Cubs play-offs all over again. We still remembered the pain of that relived over and over through highlights, even though we hadn't even watched it live because we had been too young.

But then the door to the office opened again, and a small head with neat and perfectly parted hair on top of it popped in, followed by his small impeccably dressed frame. He was holding two cans of spray paint, one red and one black, and was shaking them both up and down.

"Kitten? How did you know we were in here?"

He shrugged, staying calm, as always.

"You guys carry on with business. I'll take care of this," he said.

"Kitten, no! You'll be expelled," Vince said.

"Don't do it," I agreed. "You don't need to do this for us."

Then a sickening smile spread very slowly across Kitten's face. It was kind of like cutting open the devil and staring into the black hole where a heart should have been. Except that, in this case, the devil was on our side.

Without another word Kitten was gone, the door swinging closed.

We all sat there quietly, listening to what happened next. I heard Dickerson's muffled cry as he realized what was about to go down. Then we all heard the noise of spray-paint cans discharging. Dickerson was yelling now. Screaming, actually. I could even picture his red face with that one pulsating vein that he had in his forehead.

But even above that we heard the laughter. It had to have been Kitten's. And it sent a chill deep into my spine. That cold, maniacal laughter followed by sounds of spray paint hitting a Suit would have haunted my dreams for the rest of my life if they hadn't saved us all.

But they did save us all. So, instead, I would always remember them with a smile.

If you think this will be one of those things that you see in movies where the cool sidekick gets shot and you assume he's dead but then in the end it turns out he lived, then you're wrong. Because this is real life, not some too-good-to-be-true movie.

And the fact is that Kitten never came back after that. He was gone. That demented and glorious smile before he left Dickerson's office was the last any of us ever saw of that mad genius. I don't know what happened to him, or where he ended up, or if he's happy or sad or even still alive at all, but wherever he is, I just hope he doesn't regret what he did for us that day.

Because he really did save us all. Dickerson of course went chasing after him and likely caught him eventually. But either way the diversion bought us just enough time to finish downloading the permanent records for the entire school and vacate the area before he came back.

And because of that we made it. That's right, we actually did it. We made enough money in those six days to pay back Kinko, and we also got her the permanent records she requested.

It was time for the last phase of the mission: to have My-Me call me in sick again Tuesday morning and make the delivery. I packed the money and flash drive in an old briefcase that I borrowed from my dad's closet. And tomorrow Staples was going to drive me back out to Thief Valley.

I was so proud of everyone who had helped us. We'd all accomplished something great. The last step was simply to make it through Monday night and we'd be home free to settle this mess and finally retire once and for all.

And I'd even be able to sleep easy because we'd hired a few of the bullies to keep watch that night at my house. I mean, a lot of people from all over town knew that we'd been making a ton of money lately, so we just couldn't be too careful, especially not when we were this close to our goal.

Great White was stationed out back under my bedroom window. Little Paul was watching the front door, and Kevin patrolled the whole outside of my house. They'd all been able to sneak out easy enough that night without their parents noticing. I mean, these were trained professionals, after all. Besides, most bullies I knew didn't have parents who paid very much attention to them.

So I could sleep easy that night, and I needed it. Vince and I had worked ourselves to the bone. I mean, we'd both been getting like three or four hours of sleep each night since we'd started this effort a week ago. Which is why I fell asleep almost instantly that night. And it's also why I slept literally like a stone, a nonliving creature. I even slept through most of what followed. Which is why I also still mostly blame myself for what happened next.

# 30

## The Creek

I woke to the sounds of rustling. Or, well, I wished I could say that it was as quiet as rustling. Then I wouldn't have felt so guilty for sleeping through it. But the truth was the intruder wasn't even trying to be quiet. He was digging through my closet with reckless abandon, tossing things aside with loud clatters.

When I first woke, I was still groggy, I mean, I hadn't been sleeping very long and so I was still severely sleep-deprived. I know, I know, I'm basically making excuses now, but the fact is this: I'm still embarrassed about it all. Anyways, I was groggy, and it took me a while to react to the dark shape of a kid digging through my closet.

And then by the time I'd realized they'd found the briefcase full of cash, it took me too long to get out of bed. I stumbled and tripped over my sheets and ended up face-planting into my carpeted floor. I saw shoes run by me.

I got up and dove at the dark figure in my dark room. I missed and crashed into my desk, slamming my ribs painfully against the corner. All I could do was lie on the floor next to it, holding my aching ribs and watching as the dark figure climbed out of the window and down the slope of the roof.

I collected my breath, and the pain subsided just enough to allow me to get up. Or maybe the pain didn't subside at all, but rather the power of my anger and shock simply covered it up for the time being.

Questions coursed through my brain as I pulled on a pair of sweatpants two legs at once and then basically dove out the window after the thief. I landed on the roof and rolled to the edge, gripping the gutter and swinging down so I was hanging above the bushes below.

It was still a several-foot drop, and even with the bushes there to break my fall, there was a good chance I could shatter an ankle or femur. But those would be nothing compared to letting this punk get away with our money.

So I let go.

And it did hurt. But, thankfully, it hurt my sore ribs more than anything else when I crashed down into those shrubs. I'd gotten some scratches across my back, I was sure, but I'd avoided landing on a leg or an arm, and it didn't feel like I'd impaled myself on any of the branches, so I got up, brushed off, and looked around.

Great White was involved in a quiet struggle with two kids just as tall as he was. They must have gotten the drop on him because I was pretty sure there were no two kids in our school who Great White wouldn't be able to take on his own. The two figures were each pinning an arm, and he flailed in an attempt to get free.

"Mac!" Great White managed to get out when he saw me. "Around front. He went around front."

His attackers turned toward me momentarily. And then I saw in the pale moonlight that they were Mitch and Justin. The distraction was just enough for Great White to get an arm free, and he used it to land a right hook across Justin's stupid face. It was over now. I knew Great White had turned the table and would be able to take care of those two by himself, no problem.

So I ran in pursuit of the thief. I went around to the front yard. I saw Little Paul sitting against a tree. At first I feared that maybe he'd been knocked unconscious or worse, but as I approached him, I heard snoring. The little punk had fallen asleep on the job. But I didn't have time to deal with that just then.

I looked both ways down the street. There was no sign of Kevin, so there was really no telling what his excuse was. But I did catch a glimpse of a shadow moving behind a car a few houses down. And I wasted no time.

As I sprinted toward the car, the dark figure bolted out from behind it in the opposite direction, the briefcase full of cash tucked neatly under his left arm like a football. I was trying to see who it was, but it was hard to tell in the lighting, and in my current state.

But then I realized that the car he was just about to get into before I'd spotted him was a blue Toyota. Staples's blue Toyota.

It hit me like a slab of school meatloaf across my face. And yet, I should have known all along, really.

Staples had orchestrated the whole thing. It had been genius. First implanting himself back into my life, then utilizing the whole school rivalry and massive debt. Staples had tricked me into amassing thousands of dollars so he could steal it in one swift move. And since he'd stolen it that night instead of waiting for the exchange the next day, I'd have no proof that it was him, and I'd still technically owe Kinko the same amount of money.

She'd destroy me and the school.

Really, it had been about as brilliant a double cross as was humanly possible. Whether he was after money or revenge, he got them both.

I pushed myself as hard as I possibly could, and I was actually gaining ground. Staples made a sudden right turn and then hopped clean over a low fence like an Olympic hurdler. There was no way I could do the same, and instead I had to run around it, which gave him at least ten more yards' ground on me.

It was obvious now that the thief was headed toward The Creek, toward Vince's neighborhood. Staples's old neighborhood.

My ribs ached, my lungs felt like they were being set on fire by a mob of angry villagers with torches, and my legs and feet might as well have just been amputated because I couldn't even feel them anymore. But still I ran on, stumbling through the dark.

I mean, he was carrying at least twenty pounds of extra weight in the suitcase; he had to be just as tired as me. And I was right. As we moved our way farther toward The Creek, darting in and around trees, bushes, cars, through alleys, past barking dogs, I was gaining ground again.

Actually, I was gaining ground quickly. I thought he must have pulled something because his run was more of a hobbling limp now as he approached the Fourteenth Street bridge, a narrow two-lane road that crossed the large creek that made up the boundary, fittingly enough, of the neighborhood known as The Creek.

I was going to catch him now; that much was clear. I think he knew it, too, because he was desperately lurching forward in increasingly clumsy steps. For a second I thought he was going to fall flat on his stupid, backstabbing face.

He ran onto the bridge. The sound of the creek, which was really more like a raging river, was the only noise other than our broken and uneven footsteps. I followed him onto the bridge.

He kept running—or shuffling was probably more correct by this point. I finally caught him and grabbed the back of his hooded sweatshirt. I reached out for the case with my other hand, and he jerked it away from my grasp as he tripped and finally fell, taking me down with him.

I landed on top of him, and we both grunted. That's when I saw the airborne briefcase. It must have slipped out of his hand when he'd pulled it away from me and tripped at the same time. It soared high into the night, spinning like a Frisbee. It seemed to dangle among the stars for several seconds, as if they were trying to grab it for themselves.

All I could do was lie there on the pavement and watch helplessly as the stars finally released the brief-case and it flew right over the side railing and down into the rushing creek below.

# Chapter 31

## Defeat

**S**taples was on his feet and hobbling away down the street before I could even sit up. I didn't chase after him. For one, I was winded. And besides, what did it matter anymore? The damage was done. And even if I had caught him again, what would I do? He would beat me senseless.

I got up slowly at first, not really wanting to see the gory details down under the bridge. But then the thought of the briefcase possibly being safe and sound on the bank or still sealed and floating downstream fast practically jettisoned me onto my feet and over to the railing.

I peered over and saw the briefcase floating open

and facedown in the creek below. It was quickly rushing away downstream, but even in the darkness of night
I could see that it was a lost cause. Cash billowed out
around it in the water, becoming soggy and eventually
disappearing under the force of the black current.

The thought entered my mind briefly of running
down there and diving in to salvage what I could, but
then the idea drifted off as the briefcase rushed farther
and farther away. It was just moving too fast. I didn't
think it would even be possible to catch up with it now.
And even if I could save some of it, what would I do with
it? This was an all-or-nothing sort of situation.

I stood there silently, peering over the railing, and
watched as my fortune flowed away into the dark until
I could no longer see any trace of it. As if all four thousand dollars of it had never even existed in the first
place.

Who knows, maybe it hadn't?

That was my state of mind in that moment. I was too
shocked, too stunned, to be thinking clearly. To even
be able to tell the difference between what was real or
imagined.

I went down to the bank below and managed to salvage a few hundred dollars that had fluttered to shore
in the breeze when the briefcase opened. I still owed
money to a few of the kids who had helped me. I could

at least make good on my debt to them. Then I walked back to my house. Along the way I debated just bowing out and letting happen whatever was going to happen. I thought about just cutting my losses and staying home from school for a year, letting Jimmy dig himself out of the grave he'd dug. But the problem with that was the rest of the school would suffer, too.

And beyond that, it wouldn't be right. I mean, not necessarily because of whatever sabotage Kinko would unleash on our school, but more so just because, even after everything, I still had my business principles. I still believed there was a right way and wrong way to conduct business. And the right way was to face your own failures with some dignity and not go running away. I had made a business deal with Kinko, and it didn't matter why I wasn't able to keep my end of the deal. The fact was I hadn't kept it, and I was going to have to face the consequences. It was the right thing to do. Once I faced Kinko and took responsibility, then whatever happened after that, well, that would be out of my hands at that point.

I got back to my house to find Great White lecturing Little Paul. He was so angry that he actually had Little Paul in tears. He stopped when he saw me approaching.

"Did you catch the git?"

I nodded.

"Where's the money, then?"

I shook my head.

He strung off a whole bunch of swearwords—some that I recognized and some that were too British for me to understand, though I didn't even need to in order to know that I couldn't ever repeat them at school or in front of my parents.

"Go home," I said to Little Paul, who was sniffing and wiping frantically at his tears, trying to save face.

He nodded and hopped on his bike and pedaled away as if he was running from something.

"Where's Kevin?" I asked.

"Aw, that git ran like a bloody coward when Mitch and Justin jumped me," Great White said. "We're going to have a row about it tomorrow, me and him. Believe me."

I shrugged. I didn't really care either way anymore.

"Just don't put him in the hospital or anything, okay?" I said.

"Ay," Great White said. "Look, Mac, I'm sorry. They had the jump on me; there was nothing I could do. I tried yelling for you, but they . . . Well, it don't really matter now do it?"

I shook my head. No, it didn't. "It's okay; you're the one guy who actually did his job tonight. It's not your fault."

He nodded. "All right. Let me know if you need my

help getting even or getting out of this or something."

"Thanks," I said.

Then he got on his bike and rode off, leaving me alone in my front yard.

# Chapter 32

## Return to Thief Valley

**S**taples's car was gone the next morning when I got up. He must have come back to get it at some point. That was fine; I clearly wasn't going to catch a ride with him to TV.

Twenty minutes later, after I'd called My-Me to call me in sick again, a small car pulled in to my driveway. I got in the passenger side.

"Hey, Mac," Hannah said.

"Thanks for doing this for me," I said.

She laughed.

"I'll take any opportunity to borrow my dad's car now that I have my license. And besides, you did say you'd make it worth my while."

I laughed, too, and then handed her a twenty.

"So Thief Valley. What could you possibly have going on there?"

"It's a long story," I said, looking out the window.

"You know what? I don't think I even want to know," she said.

But I told her anyway, at least the short version.

"Well, serves you right, doesn't it?" she said as we neared Thief Valley.

"Ouch."

"I'm only kidding, Mac. But, really, I mean, if you want to keep yourself out of this kind of trouble, then you really need to let this business go. *Completely*."

I nodded. I knew that now. I just wished I had known that two months ago.

I had gotten an email from Kinko Saturday night with brief instructions on how to get into her office without setting foot on school grounds. Just to avoid the sort of recess supervisor mishap that had occurred last time. I didn't know how she got my email address, but I supposed I had my way of getting such things if I needed them, too.

Apparently most customers entered the tunnels using a secret door under the school's stage. However, some entered using a secret passage in a crawl space underneath the school janitor's equipment shed, which was located across the street from the school next to a few large industrial aluminum garages.

Kinko had told me that ten in the morning was the best time to sneak in. Her email said the janitor was usually cleaning one of the bathrooms at that time. I guessed their janitor was like most old people in that they kept to a pretty regular schedule.

I found the crawl space, then the trap door. The crawl space wasn't as dirty as you might expect, but I guessed that made sense, considering how much use it was getting. I took out the small flashlight that I'd brought and climbed down the metal ladder into a narrow cement tunnel.

It didn't take as long as I'd expected to navigate my way to the main chamber. I knocked on the steel door. It opened and I was suddenly facing the twins again. The guy smiled; the girl scowled.

"We've been expecting you," he said.

They led me inside and once again escorted me to the door of Kinko's office. The guy opened it and I stepped inside. The scene was nearly the same as last time; Kinko sat at her desk and Sue loomed behind her, leaning against a wall. But this time Michi Oba was also there, barely visible, standing in the shadows in the corner.

"Hi!" Kinko said, and then took a huge swig of Sprite.

"Hi," I said as the door behind me closed.

Kinko pointed at the chair across from her. She put the cap back on her soda and then took out a phone and started typing into it. I sat down and waited. She finished typing, paused, giggled, and then typed in something else.

"So," she said without looking up, "where's the money? It's hard to believe that you've got four grand just, like, crammed into the pockets of your jeans."

"You must already know I don't have it," I said.

She laughed, but most of her attention still seemed to be on her phone. I just sat there.

"Sorry," she said, nodding at her phone. "My friend is *so* funny."

I nodded and tried to muster a smile. If she knew about the money, maybe she'd consider taking it easy on me. She hated her brother as much as I did at that point, after all.

"Is there any way we can get a second chance?" I asked. "I mean, can you show us a little mercy? Your brother was the one who stole it from me, anyway."

She finally put her phone away.

"No, sorry," she said. "No second chances. It doesn't matter whose fault it was. What matters is that I still don't have my money or school records."

I nodded in defeat. I'd figured as much.

"We had it, though," I said. "I mean, what good is destroying our school going to do now?"

"I'm not going to destroy it," she said. "See, I own you now. You'll be making money for me until I have to pay for college. That's all I really want."

"So you want me to keep running my business and cut you in? Is that what this is now?"

"Ha! You are smart. Except not cut me in . . . I want it all. Your portion of the profits will simply be that I won't destroy your school."

She took another swig of Sprite. Then she burped. Not like you'd expect a tiny third grader to, though. Instead she let loose a huge rippling belch like you'd expect your uncle to unleash after a giant Thanksgiving dinner. Then she started giggling as if burping was the funniest thing in the world.

Even Michi Oba giggled. I shook my head. Third graders.

"So anyway, like, what were we talking about again?"

"The weather?" I suggested. "Or maybe it was football. How about those Bears, right? They're off to a good start this season."

She rolled her eyes. "So that's it, then. You'll keep running your business for me?"

The answer was simple. I couldn't go back to that life. Not after everything that had happened. It caused nothing but disaster.

"No," I said.

"Are you sure you want to say no?"

I nodded.

"You know what I can do to you and your school if I want to, right?"

I nodded again. "Still, no. I'm out. Do your worst."

"It's too bad. I kind of like you. You sort of remind me of my older brother when he was younger."

Great. That's all I needed to hear. Someday I was going to turn into a sadistic jerk who liked to punch little kids on the arm and torture them psychologically and figuratively stab them in the back.

"Thanks?" I said.

Kinko laughed and then drank more Sprite. She opened a desk drawer and pulled out a Fruit Roll-Up, which she unrolled and ate. And she ate it like you'd expect a third grader to: she flopped it around and played with the shapes and put her grimy little hands all over it first. I watched all of this in silence. Then, when she was chewing her last bite, she finally spoke again.

"Well, I probably don't even have to say how much trouble you're in. And also, I can't let you walk out of here totally scot-free either."

I tensed in my chair.

"Mark him," Kinko said.

Michi Oba started moving toward me in an instant. She was fast, faster than I'd have thought possible for a human being. I saw something large and black in her hand, and I rolled out of my chair instinctively. I got up to make a dash for it but then slammed into a wall and everything went black.

# Chapter 33

## A Wall Named Sue

I opened my eyes slowly, vaguely aware that I was sitting in what felt like a normal chair. Kinko was directly in my line of vision, and as my eyes adjusted, I saw her smirk.

"Whew, I was getting nervous!" she said.

"Did I actually run into a wall?" I asked, remembering now what had happened before I blacked out.

Kinko laughed. "You could say that, I suppose. It was probably like running into a wall. But, really, you just got introduced to Sue."

"Could have fooled me; it sure felt like a wall," I said.

Kinko giggled again. "Man, you're funny, Mac! Well, let me know when you feel good enough to walk again, and I'll have the Aussie lead you out of here."

"You're not going to mark me or whatever anymore?"

"Oh, we already did. While you were out cold."

I looked down at myself, checking for missing limbs, and then felt my torso for any holes or cuts. I seemed to be okay. Maybe she was kidding? Meanwhile, Kinko watched me panic and was giggling. Michi Oba stood behind her and grinned at me. She was missing one of her front teeth.

"What did you do to me? What is getting marked, anyway?"

Michi and Kinko looked at each other and then burst out laughing. I didn't like being toyed with. I felt my face and hair and ears, but they all felt normal, too. I decided that this just must be some sort of demented psychological mind game that they were playing.

"So I can really go? Just like that?" I asked.

"Yeah, the Aussie is outside waiting for you. He'll make sure you get off school property okay again."

"Why would you make sure I make it safely? You basically have declared open war on me and my school."

"That may be true, but I'm not going to exact revenge on my home turf. I didn't get this far by baiting the Suits like that."

I nodded. Well, she may have been an insane and

ruthless genius just like her brother, but at least she ran her business the right way. I had to respect her for that.

"What happened to you?" Hannah asked as soon as I got in her car.

"What do you mean? I'm pretty much right on time," I said.

"No, what happened to your face?" The expression of horror and shock that she had worn was wiped away by a smile. Then she started snickering.

I flipped down the visor in her car, looking for a mirror. It didn't have one. I reached out for the rearview mirror, and then Hannah smacked my hand away.

"Don't touch," she snapped.

"What did they do to my face?" I asked.

She just grinned again and shook her head.

I sighed and tried desperately to lean down in a way where I could see my face in the sideview mirror. I could see only part of it, but I could see enough to know that getting marked meant having Michi Oba draw or write stuff in thick black ink all over your face. I couldn't tell what it was exactly, but it was on my cheek, forehead, chin, everywhere.

I leaned back in my seat and let out a sigh, which Hannah answered with another laugh. But at least this one was tinged with a little sympathy, too, if that was possible.

"I can't believe you didn't tell me that the money was—Holy, what happened to your face?!" Vince said when I walked into his room that day around four o'clock.

"I got marked," I said, and sat down on his bed.

I looked in the mirror behind his bedroom door, even though I'd already had a good look when I'd gotten home earlier that afternoon. Michi was good, I'd give her that. She wrote thick black letters in a unique and eye-catching font. And they were big block letters, couldn't be missed even from a hundred miles away, probably. She had covered almost 90 percent of my face with one word written several times: *Narc*.

I'd come to find out later that that was the true art of the mark. Michi Oba had a talent. She could look at you just once and know immediately what single word you would most hate to have plastered all over your face. The one word that would probably humiliate you the most. She didn't even have to know you.

For me she'd nailed it. Especially after I'd narced myself out last year in order stop Dr. George.

"Wow. Have you tried washing it off?" Vince asked.

"No. I thought I'd leave it for a while. I kind of like it, you know?" I said.

Vince rolled his eyes. "Sorry I asked."

"No, I'm sorry, Vince. I'm just annoyed. I spent all afternoon scrubbing my face until I was pretty sure I'd turn myself into Skeletor. I don't know what kind of ink she used, but it's super permanent. How will I explain this to my parents?"

Vince shook his head and sat down on the other end of the bed. He switched on his PlayStation and handed me one of the wireless controllers. I obviously didn't feel much like video games right then, but I grabbed it anyway. Sometimes all you really need is a couple hours with a video game to make you forget about all the crappy stuff happening.

"So, what's next, then?" Vince asked as he got *Madden* going. We normally preferred baseball or FPS video games above all else, but during the first few months of the football season it was almost always the newest Madden.

I shrugged as I selected one of the worst teams. I always did since I was so much better at *Madden* than Vince. It was probably the one thing I was actually better at than him.

"Did she give any hint of what they'll do or when they'll strike?"

"No," I said.

Vince was getting frustrated. He always liked to have

a plan, to be thinking ahead. So to have no good information, I thought, was driving him crazy.

"Are we going to fight back or just let you and the school suffer?" he asked.

"I think we should just see what happens next and decide then," I said. "I mean, we've never been in this kind of spot before. I really don't know what to do."

Vince nodded. "Okay, sure. I mean, I guess it's like my grandma says . . ."

I groaned, but already I felt a smile sneaking its way onto my marked face.

"'Sometimes you just know the answer, and other times you need to wait for the arrival of Dr. Appleplasty and his team of über talented, talking lizard people.'"

And then in spite of everything else I laughed so hard I dropped my PlayStation controller, allowing Vince to score a touchdown on the first play of the game.

# Chapter 34

## The War Begins

Turns out we didn't have to wait long for Kinko to make her first move. The very next day at school a third of the kids were absent for the first few hours of the day. Turns out someone had slashed the tires of every single school bus earlier that morning in the dark. And it didn't end with just that one act, though I definitely wish it had.

Later in the morning somehow a whole section of the eighth-grade locker bay had red dye sprayed inside all of the lockers. How Kinko's crew had managed to pull that off without being seen by anyone is still a mystery to me. Luckily my locker wasn't affected, but it didn't mean I didn't still feel horrible for the kids whose lockers were. Backpacks, gym clothes, jackets, sweatshirts, homework, textbooks, all ruined. You'd have thought that the school mascot died that day or something when walking by that locker bay since so many kids were crying. It had been a pretty cruel and ruthless attack, but if that was the worst she was going to do, then maybe this wouldn't turn out so bad, after all. I mean, at the very least all of these attacks had diverted some of the attention away from my marked face. I was still getting ribbed pretty good by kids, but it would have been much, much worse without all of the other distractions.

But anyways, as you might suspect by now, those two things weren't even close to the worst things Kinko had planned for me and the school.

Later that day, around one o'clock or so, I was sitting in science class, listening to these two kids behind me argue quietly over who was going to carry whose backpack that day. They were Kate and Kiah, best friends since I could remember and the two nicest kids in the whole school. Nice to a fault, actually.

"No, I'll carry your backpack today," Kiah whispered. "I mean, your back has been sore since you hurt it at tennis practice last week."

"Kiah, don't worry about my back. I'll carry *your* bag. I mean, you're the one who broke his foot playing football this year!" Kate insisted.

"Ah, that's nothing. It's just a scratch," he said.

"A scratch? You have crutches!"

"Hey, well, okay. Why don't we carry our own bags this time, if you're going to be so stubborn? But at least let me buy you lunch today."

"But I was going to buy you lunch today! I've been planning on it all week," Kate said, her voice rising.

Luckily for them our science teacher, Mrs. Lavine, was all but deaf. One time a kid mixed together some chemicals he shouldn't have and the resulting explosion actually shattered three of the classroom windows, and Mrs. Lavine didn't even turn around. She just kept on writing stuff on the board.

"Shoot, what are we going to do?" Kiah said.

"We can vote?" suggested Kate. "That's the most diplomatic way."

Kiah laughed quietly. "But our votes always end in a one-to-one tie!"

"Maybe this time will be different?" Kate said.

I tried not to barf all over myself. Of all the people I ended up sitting next to, why did it have to be them? Everybody usually got pretty annoyed with them. We all kept saying that they should just stop messing around and get married already, since it was obvious that's what was going to happen eventually. Except they'd probably argue more than any married couple on the planet, despite also being the nicest to each other. Well, this was mostly based on my own parents and movies, but whatever.

Around the time they were about to start counting their votes and would inevitably reach another one to one stalemate, they stopped talking. The whole class did. Instead we listened to the trickling sound that was growing louder and louder, the same sound the creek had made the night it mercilessly swallowed up four thousand dollars of hard-earned cash.

Then kids in the front row started leaping from their desks. Mrs. Lavine was still involved in grading some quizzes and hadn't yet realized that *something* was happening. Those of us near the back never had the luxury of being able to react in time to avoid damage because all of the kids jumping around on their chairs and desks in front of us blocked our view and distracted us.

I didn't figure out what the deal was until I felt my feet were suddenly engulfed in cold liquid. The other kids in the back started leaping from their desks, only making the splashing worse. I, however, just sat there and let the water gushing in from under the classroom door swirl around my ankles.

By the time Mrs. Lavine had figured out that her feet were in eight inches of water, the flowing had stopped and now the water just pooled there, cold and smelly and slightly yellowish, obviously the act of a master saboteur.

They dismissed us from the school for the rest of the day while they investigated what exactly had happened to cause the whole school to flood and also to start the clean-up process. Vince and I walked home that day together, and while we both agreed that it was likely Kinko who was responsible, what we couldn't figure out was why.

I mean, all the incident had done was ruin some shoes and get all of our students a free half day off from school, maybe even more. What was her angle?

By the next day—on which school was canceled again—we found out. And it cemented Kinko, in my mind at least, as the most diabolical and genius saboteur in history. The act, which had seemed subtly good at first, ended up being the ultimate sucker-punch. Which I'm sure was exactly the intent.

School was canceled for the next three days while they tried to clean the place up, fix the pipes, and test for mold. Which, like I said, seemed awesome. But it wasn't. There are state laws that require all students get a certain amount of school hours every year. So we now had to make up the time missed either at the end of the year or during winter break.

So just like that, she'd cost us three days of our

already limited precious holiday break. And the rumor was that the incident had caused so much damage and would be so expensive to fix that the school was basically flat-out broke now and might have to cut a few programs, including several spring sports and over a dozen school clubs.

If our school had been a living, breathing person, then Kinko had basically just shot it in the gut with a shotgun with a debilitating disease all over the ammo. Okay, that's kind of morbid, sure, but so was an entire school having to tromp through our own sewer water for half a day.

Furthermore, Ears, my best informant, told me he heard that Dickerson knew it was an act of sabotage. But he assumed it was an inside job. And that I was at the top of the suspect list. The word was that Dickerson would be gunning for me when school resumed that Thursday.

And that's when I realized exactly what Kinko's game was. She was going to destroy me and my school in a single diabolical move. This wasn't business, this was personal.

# Chapter 35

## Pulled Back In

I held my nose closed from the musty stench of the recently flooded, old building as Dickerson led me into his office on Thursday morning. He'd personally come to my first-hour class to escort me. That was never a good sign.

"What happened to your face?" he said as he sat down.

"Oh, just a joke some friends played on me," I said, trying to sound casual. The ink had started to fade, thankfully, but it was still plenty visible.

I could tell from Principal Dickerson's expression that he didn't find the "joke" very funny at all. In fact, he was disgusted by it.

"I knew you hadn't changed," he said.

"But I didn't do this!" I said, pointing at my face. "Why would I?"

"I don't know what sorts of gang rituals you kids have these days. So who knows?"

"*Gang rituals?*" I said. "Mr. Dickerson, I never—"

"I know you're up to something again, Christian," he interrupted. "Those pipes didn't burst on their own. That red ink didn't just come from nowhere. Not to mention the whole fleet of school buses getting their tires slashed. Do you have any idea how much all of this has set us back? We're going to have to lay off some teachers! Do you really want that on your conscience? If you even have one?"

"I swear I had nothing to do with this!" I said, which wasn't entirely true.

"Why would I ever believe you anymore?" he said.

I didn't know how to answer that convincingly so I just shrugged.

"Well, just know this, Christian. The school board determined that the pipe incident was 'accidental,' even though I *know* better. But I'm telling you, the next time anything, and I mean *anything*, 'funny' happens around here like the red-ink locker bay incident that I know was a deliberate act, you're taking the fall for it. And you'll be expelled immediately. Vince, too."

"But you can't just . . . I mean, you need proof!"

"Not when a student has a history like yours, I don't," he said.

I could see, thankfully, that he was taking no pleasure in this. In fact, it was likely that his hands were tied. I mean, considering what our school had been through, he was probably under a ton of pressure from the Higher-Up Suits to put an end to this type of activity here. And so his hand was being forced. I could hardly blame him, even as unfair as it was.

"I haven't been doing any of this, though," I pleaded.

"One. More. Incident. That's it, dismissed."

I got up and left feeling pretty helpless. I mean, now my choices were:

Do nothing, wait for another attack, and then get expelled.

Fight back, underestimate Kinko once again, and get the snot beat out of me by Sue and Michi Oba and then Staples, and then probably get expelled for good measure.

Start working for Kinko like she'd asked and then definitely get expelled and probably get the snot beat out of me afterward for kicks.

Beg for mercy.

And so, at lunch that day Vince and I went to the computer lab to type an email to Kinko. Option four was about all we had left. Vince was a much better writer, so he helped me, and together we came up with what I thought was a pretty professional and thoughtful email.

In it we explained to Kinko my predicament, explained how badly she had crippled the school. Expressed that we all knew she was superior. But that doing anything further wouldn't ever get me to work for her. All it would do was ruin the school year of a bunch of kids and maybe even the lives of some teachers. And then at the end we hinted that if any further action was taken against us, we'd have nothing else to lose by waging war right back. I thought, all things considered, that she'd be stupid not to accept the truce. It made perfect sense to me. She really had nothing more to gain by continuing this any further.

We clicked Send.

Now all we could do was wait.

After school Vince and I went back to the computer lab. iBully was there, as usual, working on some top-secret coding project. I nodded at him, and he flicked a quick wave in my direction, never taking his eyes off the screen.

I logged into my email and saw the reply right away. Kinko had replaced the subject line with a smiley-face emoticon.

"Vince, I think she went for it!" I said.

Vince grinned and nodded. "Well, what are you wait-ing for, open it!"

I clicked the email. Instantly my computer screen turned blue. In fact, all of the screens in the lab did. Then words started flashing on the screen in bold green letters, one at a time.

YOU

ARE

GOING

DOWN

PUNK

!!!!!!!

LOVE,

KINKO

On the last screen with her name on it there were also hearts and smiley faces and an animated flower that was dancing on the back of a unicorn.

This had happened on every computer in the lab. Then the screens all flashed black, and a white ani-mated skull appeared and it looked like it was laughing. Then everything went dark.

"Holy, Mac. She sent a virus to the whole school!" Vince said.

iBully wheeled his chair over, looking panicked.

"No, no, no, that's not possible," he said as he started typing frantically at my computer. "I set up all the extra security myself. The system was hack-proof . . . well, except by me, of course."

iBully sat there and typed madly for at least fifteen minutes, the whole time muttering technical mumbo-jumbo to himself like, "Wire access net compromised" or "Cnet drive isn't found; how is that possible?" or "Server failure at code zero zero seven?"

Of course I had no idea what he was saying, but all in all it didn't sound good.

It must have affected the whole school, because by that time the school's computer teacher and tech guy, Mr. Kilmer, was in the lab, watching iBully go. Even he knew that iBully was the only person who could possibly fix this.

iBully was able to get the screen from pitch-black to blue with some text on it and eventually to a green screen with some text, but in the end he never could get it back to a normal Windows screen. After twenty minutes more he pushed back from his table and looked at us, dazed.

"They did it," he said.

"What?" Mr. Kilmer demanded. "Did what?"

"They took us out," iBully said. "I've never seen work so advanced. They wiped out the whole system. All my years of hard work, gone, all of it. Backup servers, too. It's all gone forever."

He got up slowly. He stumbled toward the door, barely able to walk.

Mr. Kilmer went after him. "Wait, wait, what do you *mean*? It's *all* gone? Grades, school records, all of it? Are you sure they got to the backup servers? How is that possible?"

I saw iBully nod slowly as they exited the computer lab. I looked at Vince. He looked at me.

For once, there was nothing to say.

# Chapter 36

## Expulsion

I knew it was bad when I went down to the administration offices the next morning after getting called in and saw my parents there. My mom was crying.

If you think this was like last time where I could talk my way out of it, you're wrong. This time it was official. It was a "done deal," or so Dickerson said several times during our meeting.

I was hereby expelled from Thomas Edison Elementary and Middle School.

I tried to argue that I hadn't planted the virus, but Dickerson said it didn't matter. They were still able to trace it to my school email account, and that was enough since I had already been warned numerous times that year, which, in all honesty, was the truth. The school board had already approved the decision and signed the papers.

The only good news was that I had managed to convince Dickerson to let Vince stay in school. I signed this thing called an affidavit stating that Vince was in no way involved in the email exchange that caused the computer system meltdown.

The school didn't let me go back to class to get my stuff or even to my locker to get my jacket. They said all of that would be mailed to me later that week. We were escorted out immediately. On the way out I saw Mr. Kjelson, who'd I'd really been looking forward to having as a baseball coach later that school year. And now it would never happen.

He gave me a somber head nod as we passed. I tried to smile, but all I managed was a lip quiver. I forced myself not to cry.

The car ride home was the longest of my life. My parents didn't even talk to me. Never before had they had absolutely nothing to say to me. Not even last year when I'd confessed to cheating on the SMARTs for the entire school.

When we got home, they still didn't say anything. My

dad just pointed upstairs. We all knew I was going to be grounded forever; that much was obvious.

I went up to my room and lay on my bed. Well, at least one thing had become much clearer now: there'd be no pulling our punches anymore. I was going to eliminate Kinko's whole operation for good.

My parents had taken my phone from me first thing when we'd left the school that day. But what they didn't know was that Vince and I kept a pair of long-range walkie-talkies hidden in our rooms for use in just these types of situations.

At 3:45 p.m., when I was sure that he'd be home, I contacted him via our emergency channel. He must have been anticipating it, because he answered right away.

"I can't believe it" was the first thing he said.

"I know," I said as quietly as I could.

"I heard about you sparing me," he said. "You should have let him expel me. Then we could still go to school together wherever you'll end up."

"No, you need Kjelson this year. He's the only coach good enough for you. Besides, there'd be no way to know that we'd end up at the same school."

I thought he knew I was right because there was a long silence. Then finally he spoke again.

"It's like my grandma says, 'This—sucks.'"

There was static on the line and I couldn't hear the middle word, but I was pretty sure I knew what it was.

For once Grandma had nailed it.

"Anyways, Vince, I was contacting you to tell you to get in touch with Tyrell, Great White, and the Beagle. There's only one thing left to do, and that's to get revenge and save the school. This time, it's war."

That night we called a secret meeting in my basement after my parents fell asleep. The planning went well, with pretty good contributions from everybody.

"What about you?" Vince said. "How will you get out? I'm sure your parents will be keeping tabs on you."

"Don't worry about it," I said. "I've gotten out while grounded hundreds of times. This will be no different. They're basically ignoring me, they're so mad anyway."

"What about getting to Thief Valley tomorrow? We obviously can't ask Staples. My brother is away in college now. . . . My mom will be working. We can't call a cab; it'll be too suspicious. . . ."

"Vince, I got it covered, pal. Are we all good?"

Great White, Tyrell, and the Beagle all nodded and got up to leave. Vince hung back for a minute after they all walked out.

"Mac, I . . . I just can't believe you won't be my catcher

this year. I need you back there, man."

I was getting choked up thinking about it. Seriously.

Vince must have been in the same boat because he simply turned and left and that was that.

# Chapter 37

## Facing the Enemy

We all met the next morning at nine at Vince's like we'd discussed the night before. Everyone showed up right on time, and they all had their supplies in their backpacks. Except for the Beagle, our school's animal and science expert. He had two huge duffel bags with small holes punched in them. Knowing what was inside made me shudder.

"Okay, so how are we getting there?" Vince asked.

I'd had My-Me call us all in sick that day—except for me, obviously. I just had to sneak out. My dad had finally talked to me. He stopped by that morning to say that they'd be home periodically to make sure I wasn't burning the place down or torturing any small animals. I was a little hurt by the comments, but it was hard to blame him for having that attitude. After all, when he came by to check on me later, I wouldn't be there. Instead I'd be out causing more trouble. I was just starting to fully realize the consequences of the life I'd chosen. Running a business like mine had come with so much more baggage than it'd seemed like at first. Only now when it was too late did I fully get that.

Anyways, it wouldn't look suspicious for the rest of them all to be absent at the same time since none of them were really friends in school. We were all business partners, for the most part, but not much else. That said, the lines had become blurred over the years, I had to admit. Even the ruthless Great White was really growing on me.

"Well?" Vince repeated. "Where's our transport?"

"She should be here soon," I said, and glanced at my watch.

Then as if on cue, a small car pulled into Vince's driveway. Hannah Kjelson got out of the driver's side, looking nervous.

"No way," Vince said in awe.

"You know where to drop them off?" I said.

Hannah nodded.

"Them?" Vince said. "You're not going?"

"I'll meet you guys there later. There's something I want to do first. You go and get the plan in motion as scheduled."

Vince nodded and then got into the car, followed by the others. That's why I love Vince: he knew that sometimes it was best to not ask questions. He trusted that I had a good reason.

"So you'll pick me up downtown in like forty minutes?" I said to Hannah.

She gave me a thumbs-up and then got into her car and drove away. I hopped onto Vince's bike and took off in the opposite direction.

I got to Staples's apartment building about fifteen minutes later. He'd had us over a few times to watch football and eat chili and nachos. "Classic Big Brother," he'd said at the time. What a load of crap.

I didn't need to buzz for him because as I pulled up, I saw him walking toward his garage. I pedaled after him and then drove around and stopped right in front of him.

"Mac! Where were you Tuesday morning? I waited at the pickup spot forever! And what's up with you and Vince not answering my calls or texts? I mean, what is going on?"

He had been calling both Vince and me and sending us text messages. We'd been deleting them all unread. I didn't need to read his gloating.

"Right," I said. "Like you're going to play dumb?"

"Play dumb about what?"

"Look, I know it was you who stole our money! We trusted you! We thought you really had turned yourself around. And it turns out it was all a lie, another lie. You were double-crossing us from the start!"

"Mac," Staples said, holding up his hands. "What the heck are you talking about?"

"I know you took advantage of everything going on with your sister's business to steal a ton of cash and take revenge on us for what happened last year. That's why I came here, to tell you what we're doing to your sister's business as we speak. I wanted to see your face when you found out."

"My sister's business?" He was practically shouting now. "Wait. Kinko is my *sister*?"

I'd never seen a look of surprise and shock on a person's face like I did on Staples's right then.

I took a step back. He really didn't know . . . but how was that possible? How was any of this possible? Then who was the thief? Why was Staples's car there that night?

"You better start explaining yourself," he said with his fist balled up at his side, ready to knock teeth out of some poor fool's jaw. Mine, to be specific.

So I did. I recapped everything that had happened since Tuesday.

"Unbelievable," he said. "You're an idiot."

"But how could I have known? I mean, your car was there!"

"That wasn't my car, Mac! Don't you realize that there are like nine billion blue Toyota Corollas roaming the streets? That one is always parked down the street from you. I pointed it out almost every time we drove past it!"

"I . . ." I started, but what was there to say? He was right; I was an idiot.

"What's this about your plan today, huh? You said you wanted to see my face when you told me what you were doing."

I told him about our planned attack on Kinko and her school, which was happening right now.

"Oh man, I have to go help my sister."

He ran to his garage and drove off before I could barely get a word out, let alone catch him. He was fast. How had I ever thought that the thief had been Staples? Staples was way too athletic to ever let a seventh grader catch him, cramp or no cramp.

Waiting for Hannah to show up was excruciating. I had to get to the school. I had to fix this before Staples barged in to TV Elementary and got himself arrested. Thankfully Hannah showed up right on time, just a few minutes after Staples had left.

# Chapter 38

## Battle Royale

**D**uring the drive I could barely sit still. What had I done? I knew better, but I had let my anger at getting expelled get the better of me. And now I was about to make everything worse. I wished I still had my phone so I could call Vince and call off the hit.

Thankfully Hannah drove like a maniac, so when we pulled up at the school, Staples was just on his way toward the front door and not inside already. I hopped out and ran up to him.

"Staples, don't!" I yelled.

He turned. "I've got to help Abby!"

"If you go in there, you'll never get her back. Wait here. I'll go in. I can fix this."

Staples scowled at me but then nodded and stomped back toward his car. He leaned against it and then slid down until he was sitting on the pavement with his back to the driver's-side door. He stuck his face in his hands and slumped forward.

I went around the school to the back. I went through the secret entrance to the tunnels that Kinko had told me about in her email last week. As soon as I got down there, I realized I was too late.

The first thing I saw in the main chamber was the Beagle, running from tunnel entrance to tunnel entrance, releasing several small snakes into each one as we'd planned.

"Go, my lovelies!" he said. "This tunnel looks perfect for an *Elaphe obsoleta quadrivittata*. Yes, indeed. Oh, and this one is just right for Gary, the *Elaphe guttata guttata*."

I was getting the willies already just thinking about snakes in those dark tunnels. Tyrell had slipped off somewhere like I figured he would. I knew that if I couldn't see him, he still could probably see me.

Vince and Great White were involved in a skirmish with the twins. Then the door to Kinko's office burst open.

Sue came charging out, followed by a black blur. And then Kinko stood right in the doorway, grinning.

"Let's do this," she said, pulling out a thick yardstick and wielding it like a sword.

"Wait, stop!" I shouted.

But no one heard me.

Beagle dashed into the room and emptied the last of the small snakes, which he had assured me were not poisonous or overly aggressive, onto the floor.

"Go, be free, my small army of *Lampropeltis triangulum elapsoides*! Do my bidding!" The Beagle held up his hands as dozens of snakes writhed their way across the floor, slithering over one another like they were all part of one single being. He cackled madly.

Kinko screamed and took a step back. Even Sue, the huge monster that he was, stopped dead in his tracks. Only the black blur known as Michi Oba seemed unfazed. She darted from person to person striking out with her black marker in quick strokes.

I saw that she'd already somehow managed to write a whole swearword on Vince's left cheek. He'd have a doozy of a time explaining that one to his mom and teachers later.

Kinko regrouped and started swinging her yardstick at the snakes, which sent Beagle diving to protect them while screaming out their names. I had no idea how he could tell them apart.

"No, Sleepy! I'll protect you! How dare you swing at

Mr. Conley!" he yelled, cowering over the snakes and taking repeated blows to his back from the yardstick.

Vince scrambled tentatively through the swarm of slithering snakes on the floor toward Kinko so he could help Beagle. Meanwhile, Sue and Great White were now engaged in a battle in the middle of the room. Great White, although clearly outmatched by the monster size-wise, was doing just enough to get in Sue's way and keep him busy. Part of that involved Great White slugging Sue in the torso and stomach repeatedly. The punches seemed to be bouncing off with little effect, but they had to be adding up.

Then I heard faint screams behind me, getting closer.

"Snakes, snakes, snakes, snakes!" the voice shouted as it grew louder. The Aussie came shooting out of the tunnels with a small snake in his hair and more slithering out behind him. "Snakes in the tunnels!"

It was total chaos now. I saw Kinko whack Vince in the face with her yardstick, and then I spotted Michi Oba marking a section of the wall. A section of the wall that then moved and yelled out in surprise.

Except that she wasn't marking the wall at all, obviously; she was marking Tyrell. She'd spotted him, no problem. I couldn't believe it. He'd finally met his match.

I kept yelling for everyone to stop, but it was no use. It was an all-out battle. Then suddenly I was tackled from behind. I hit the hard ground with a grunt.

"This will teach you," my attacker said, driving a knee into my lower back.

I rolled and kicked, managing to clip him in the ankle. He stumbled and nearly fell. I reached out and grabbed his ankles and pulled until he did hit the deck. Then I recognized who it was.

"Jimmy?" I said. "What are you doing here?"

"You mean you haven't figured it out yet, guy?"

"You! You stole the money!"

I couldn't believe I had been so blind. Of course. Jimmy and Kinko had been in on this together the whole time. It all made sense now. Jimmy was too good a businessman to let things get as out of control as they did . . . unless he let them on purpose. They had played me and I had let them.

"Wow, way to go, genius. It only took you forty billion years to figure it out."

He climbed to his feet and charged at me again. I rolled away, and he went sprawling on the ground. That's when I grabbed one of the snakes and let it slither up his pant leg. He screamed, scrambled to his feet, and ran out of the chamber through the passage that led to the shed entrance outside.

I heard a battle cry and turned around. Kinko was charging right at me with her yardstick swinging around over her head like a propeller. I turned and also ran through the tunnel.

She was four years younger than me, sure, but she was also insane and wielding a heavy yardstick.

I went up through the tunnel and into the maintenance shed that housed the secret tunnel entrance. Jimmy was outside already, still jumping around trying to shake the snake free.

Kinko was still right behind me, and I had to duck as she followed me out, swinging madly.

The snakes must have been getting to everyone, because it wasn't long before the fight had moved almost entirely outside. It was chaos: Sue and Great White and Vince and the two twins were in a pile of fists and kicks and it was hard to tell who, if anyone, was winning. But then a loud voice of authority froze us all.

"What is going on out here?"

"Principal Cochran!" one of the twins yelled.

I turned and saw a middle-aged lady with a distinctly principal-ian vibe flanked by two teachers.

"Run!" I shouted.

Vince and Great White broke away from the pack and started running. One of the teachers went after them. I stayed back. I didn't care what happened to me now. I just needed to make sure I could get as many of the others out of this as I could.

Principal Cochran grabbed Kinko's arm, and the other teacher corralled Sue and Jimmy. Michi Oba, the Beagle, and Tyrell were nowhere to be seen.

"What is the meaning of this, Abby Larson?" Principal Cochran shouted. "And what were you doing down in the tunnels? You know that entering those tunnels is an automatic suspension! Maybe we should go down there and see what you've been up to?"

"No!"

I turned. It was Staples. He must have heard the fighting from the front of the school.

"Pardon?" Principal Cochran said.

Staples walked up to her and shook his head.

"No, it was me. I'm sorry. Don't punish her for something that was my idea. I had left things of mine down there from years back and paid these kids to go down after them for me. They didn't have any idea what they were getting themselves into. And Abby didn't have anything to do with it."

"Staples," I started. If he took the fall for this, then he could kiss his chances at getting custody of his sister good-bye.

"Shut up, Mac," he said, turning back to Principal Cochran. "My sister hasn't had anyone to stick up for her in her entire life. Don't punish her for things I did years ago. This is my fault."

He looked at Kinko and she looked away. Her head was down, her hair swinging over her face. I saw a clear drop fall and land on her shoe.

"Well, you always were my *favorite* former student, Barry," Mrs. Cochran said dryly. "I was hoping I'd never have to see you again. I have to say I'm not surprised that you're behind all this."

Just then the other teacher who had chased Vince and Great White came walking back toward us, alone. He was breathing hard and shaking his head. They had gotten away.

"Well, come on, all of you, let's go sort this out," Mrs. Cochran said. "Abby, since it seems you're a bystander in all this, I'd like you to head back to class with Mr. Erickson. I'll be calling your foster parents to let them know what's happening."

Everyone started heading back toward the building, one of the teachers rounding up me and Sue and the twins and the rest of the kids from Thief Valley.

I probably could have made a break for it right then, but I figured what's the point? I really sort of deserved whatever I had coming to me. Just like Staples, I guess. I had no one to blame but me and I deserved whatever punishment I got. Besides, what would they do to me? I was already expelled.

As we all walked back toward the school, I saw Kinko

nudging her way closer and closer to Staples until she was right next to him. Then she reached out her small hand and took Staples's. He looked down at her, and I saw his red, tear-filled eyes. And then he held her hand back. She grabbed his arm and leaned her head against it as they walked.

Two schools had been trashed. Thousands of dollars lost. I had been expelled, and would likely be grounded for life. And there was no telling what would happen to Staples and the rest of my friends.

But suddenly, for just a moment, everything seemed just as it should be.

# Epilogue

**Y**ou didn't seriously think this was just going to end without me filling you in on how everything turned out, did you? You ought to know me better than that by now.

Well, as it turned out, we did suffer some casualties that day at TV Elementary. The Beagle had stayed behind in the tunnels to gather up all of his snakes. Supposedly he just kept yelling, "I shall leave no *Serpentes/Ophidia* behind! I shall save you all!" as he scrambled into the tunnels to find them. So, as a result, he got caught and was eventually expelled, just like me.

I felt pretty horrible about it for a while, but the Beagle assured me he didn't care. He said over and over that he'd rather get expelled saving his snakes than get away clean but lose just one of them. Plus, he seemed pretty proud that he'd joined the ranks of me and Kitten as local legends for sacrificing ourselves for the greater good. The Beagle deserved to feel proud of what he had done that day. Without his snakes and the chaos they had caused, the fight never would have moved outside. And then who knows what would have happened?

Another casualty was Tyrell. Michi Oba had schooled him, basically. And while he managed to escape mostly in one piece and without getting detention or being expelled, he definitely had left his pride and dignity behind. He got marked something awful. I mean, it was just the name Roger Moore written on his face over and over again, which I didn't understand, but to Tyrell it was pretty much the end of the world to have that name labeled all over his face for three weeks. Especially in conjunction with getting bested by a small grade schooler.

So Tyrell actually retired and went into hiding shortly after our raid. He said he needed to do it in order to "regain his confidence and restore himself in the ranks of spies." Whatever that meant.

Anyways, I'd give it even money that he and Michi Oba would eventually cross paths again. There will be no way to tell. After all, good spies are only seen when they want to be seen.

Great White and Vince got roughed up pretty good during the brawl, and they both got marked as well. Great White was marked with the words "Manchester United," which about killed him. He just kept telling me, "But, Mac, I'm from Liverpool! Liverpool! I can't have this rubbish on my face!"

Vince was marked with the word "smug." Man, did he hate having that word on his face. Pretty much the opposite of what he was. Michi Oba clearly had no equal.

So, anyways, who's to say that all of this doesn't repeat itself, right? With Jimmy and Kinko going right back to what they were doing? Well, Jimmy Two-Tone also was caught for the incident. Apparently this wasn't his first run-in with trouble because his parents sent him off to some military academy.

Kinko, though, had no desire to go back into business. She had been running it in the first place to prove to Staples that she could take care of herself, that she didn't need him anymore. Which was sort of not true at all, it turned out.

And as for the Fourth Stall? Well, Dickerson got so sick of all these horrible things happening to our school that he actually scrounged up enough money to get a real toilet installed in there. He also had the bathroom cleaned up and restored to meet all health codes. So, as of today, the East Wing boys' bathroom is once again a fully functioning bathroom and nothing more. At least as far as I know.

And then there was Staples. Well, taking the fall for his sister really did kill his case to get legal custody of her. But he'd won back her affection and as he told me, that was the real first step. More important than Big Brother programs and nice haircuts, he realized.

And he was right. After a six-month deferred sentence with perfect behavior, Staples was once again able to plead his case to the court. And this time Kinko actually testified that she wanted nothing more than to go live with her brother. Which is why I'm happy to report that he eventually did get legal custody of his sister. Apparently they moved away not too long ago, and I just hope they don't someday team up and form the ultimate nightmare of a brother/sister duo. I'm only kidding. I'm sure they're both retired for good. Or, well, I hope they are anyway.

So that just leaves Vince and me, right? Well, soon after the raid on Thief Valley, my parents sent me to this stupid behavioral reformation camp out in the woods in Oregon for six weeks. No, seriously, they did.

And man, those kids I was stuck in the wilderness with were nuts. We had some insane, insane adventures up in those hills and forests. I mean, first there was the wolverine incident, and then the fact that Crazy Ronnie kept trying to start his tent on fire with a laser, and that's not even half as crazy as when a group of us got separated from the chaperones (or "behavior reformation counselors") for two weeks. Then, most insane of all was . . . Well, actually, you know what? These stories are way too long to tell here. But let me just say, I survived . . . barely, and that's what matters.

Anyways, after I got back from that ordeal, my parents were able to get me into a private school nearby. So we didn't have to move, which was great. Because of my expulsion, though, I had to repeat seventh grade! Which completely sucks, needless to say. It's pretty embarrassing, but I did it all to myself in a way, so what could I do?

At first it was excrutiating to not have Vince at school with me. But then after a few weeks we both got used to it. I mean, sure Vince is still my absolute best friend without a doubt. But I have some new pals at my new school, and Vince and I still hung out almost every day after school. And we still watched every Cubs game we could together.

Probably the hardest part and the one thing we'd never get used to was that he had a new catcher now. The good news is that Vince was the seventh-grade team's ace, even without me. And he shattered almost every single-season pitching record in our school history. But

I had fun watching him play and he deserved all the accolades in the world for pretty much being the best and coolest human being alive.

And next year, if I can make the team at my new school, I'll even get to face Vince in a few games. Which ought to be kinda fun, as long as he doesn't give me any chin music. Which, honestly, he might. Vince is the nicest guy in the whole world off the field, but once he's on the mound in a game situation, he's like a bulldog. He doesn't back down and he'll do anything he can (as long as it's mostly legal) to win.

So, anyways, that only leaves one question left unanswered, right? Did I finally get to retire, or am I up to my old schemes again at my new school? Well, it turned out there were more ways to get out of the business than juvie or a body bag. The third way was to change schools. Most of the kids at my new school didn't know who I was, which made it a lot easier to avoid getting drawn into other kids' problems.

I mean, I have to admit I've been tempted a few times, but in all reality I don't think I can survive another round of the crap I just went through the past few years. So I'm staying retired. Definitely, for sure, staying retired. No way am I going back to that. Absolutely zero chance.

I mean, at least until high school. Because in high

school kids have jobs and that means way more money and way more problems. From what I've heard, just a simple zit is enough to cause mass rioting.

And that's pretty much where I come in.

TURN THE PAGE FOR A SNEAK PEEK
AT THE FIRST BOOK IN
CHRIS RYLANDER'S NEXT SERIES

THERE I WAS IN THE PARKING LOT OF MY SCHOOL, MINDING my own business, when some mysterious dude shows up and hands me an even more mysterious package. Okay, so I wasn't so much minding my own business as I was putting the finishing touches on the fourth biggest prank in Erik Hill Middle School history. But the point was the same—I was busy. I didn't really have time to talk to this guy who'd just run up to me as if he were in the middle of a race with his own shadow. Sweat poured down his face and he was breathing so hard I thought he was going to literally cough up a chunk of his lung onto one of my brand-new sneakers.

The sweating and panting itself wasn't all that strange—I mean, lots of weirdos like to go for runs. But just not usually in a black business suit and tie at 2:55 in the afternoon on a 100-degree day with a sun so blazing that lizards were melting on sidewalks all over town. At least his black sunglasses actually fit the sunny situation.

"Hey, kid," the guy said.

I tried to ignore him, because like I said, I was busy. But he was persistent.

"Hey!" he said again, frantically grabbing my arm.

"What?" I asked.

"Take this."

Suddenly I was holding a package. It was about the size of a shoe box but only half as thick. And it was wrapped in plain brown paper with no markings of any kind on it and clear tape holding the folds in place. The wrapping was tight and neat, the same way my mom likes to basically suffocate Christmas presents when she wraps them. It was clean, too, except for the damp spots where his sweaty fingers had touched it.

My first thought was that someone was playing a prank on me. I should know; I'd done my share of them over the years. In fact, counting the one I was about to execute, I would now be responsible for the all-time top five pranks in school history. But there was something about the guy's desperate and almost terrified look that kept me from laughing at him and handing the package back.

"What am I supposed to . . . ?"

"Just listen," he said, while glancing over both shoulders quickly. "You must guard this with your life; the fate of the world depends on it. And whatever you do, don't open it!"

"What?"

He flipped a finger under the lens of his sunglasses and wiped away a stream of sweat. "You must deliver this to Mr. Jensen. It must go *only* to Mr. Jensen, you understand? Trust no one."

He didn't get a chance to say anything more because at that moment the school bell rang. Our school still had a bell on the outside of it that rang every day at 3:00 when school was out. And on this particular day, it also signaled my friend, Dillon, to initiate the first phase of the prank. So when the bell rang, chaos broke out.

I turned back to the guy to ask him again what I was supposed to do with the package, but he was no longer there. He was running away from me, across the parking lot toward Sixteenth Street. He ran right by the stream of goats that was headed toward the school's front entrance. And now two guys with painted white faces were chasing him.

I didn't have time to wonder who he was, where he was going, or where the guys with the white faces had come from. Because shortly after the bell rang, kids started filing out of the school. That was my cue to get the heck out of there.

Also, that's when the herd of fainting goats reached the front entrance of the school.

If you've never seen a fainting goat in action, you're missing out. They're one of the few things in North Dakota worth seeing. Basically it's this breed of goat that faints when they get scared. And they serve no other practical purpose, even to a farmer, which in my book makes them about the most perfect animal in the world. All they do is eat grass and faint.

But today they had an actual purpose. Or several. For one, hundreds of goats running and fainting all over a school lawn at 3:00 was just plain hilarious to see, especially when your school's mascot is Gordy, the Fighting Billy Goat. But more important, the chaos they'd create would provide a big enough distraction for me to execute the real prank. One that involved something very simple: glue.

That's right, glue. I mean, gluing a teacher's computer mouse to their desk was a classic. Nothing new there, I get it. But what about if it were taken to a new, ridiculous level? Such as supergluing every single door in the school shut? Including the principal's? And that would be only after gluing down all the items on his desk, of course. Plus we'd glue all the items on all the other teachers' desks. And all the lockers in the locker room, all the science supplies in the storeroom, all the mops and brooms in the maintenance closets, everything. Basically the whole school would be on Glue-Down. Incapacitated when the day started tomorrow. That's what made the goats so purposeful today. Simply pulling the fire alarm wouldn't work since teachers had to then make sure that all kids exited the building before they did. But a whole herd of fainting goats? Well, for that, the school would simply empty altogether in an attempt to control the situation with no regard for who snuck back in or stayed behind to do whatever their hearts desired.

So, basically, it was pandemonium . . . or goatemonium is probably a better word for it. There were goats running and yelling, kids running and yelling, and then the goats started fainting. Teachers started coming outside to see what the commotion was, which led to more yelling and goats fainting. I even saw one goat chewing on a teacher's pant leg right before it fainted, the pants still clutched in its jaws as it went rigid and fell over.

Everything was going exactly as planned. My best friends, Dillon and Danielle, and our usual accomplices, Zack and Ethan, were probably already splitting up into the various areas of the school, gluing stuff down wherever they found it. And I should have been inside already, too, helping them with Principal Gomez's office before he got suspicious and headed back inside the school himself.

But I wasn't inside gluing.

All because of the sweaty guy in the suit. I was still standing there, mostly watching the pale-faced guys chase the sweaty dude in the black suit. Right at the corner of Sixteenth and Burdick the two pasty weirdos caught him. One tackled him right onto the pavement. And I saw, even as kids laughed and screamed and goats were fainting all around me, their legs sticking straight up in the air like upside-down tables, that a black sedan had stopped next to the three men. Another guy in a suit jumped out and helped the pasty dudes shove the former package bearer inside the car.

That's also when I saw the guns in their hands.

And one of them looked right at me before he got into the car. I could have sworn, even at that distance and even among the fainting, petrified goats and screaming kids and parents honking their car horns and teachers trying to calm everyone down, that he saw me holding the package. But then they all piled into the car and it sped off and I was left there, holding this thing and staring right at the principal, who had come out of nowhere.

Mr. Gomez scowled at me in that way that only principals can.

"Mr. Fender. My office. Right now."

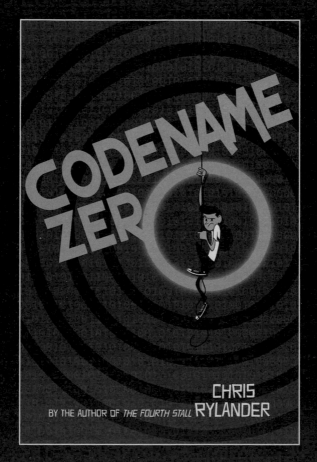